# The Brothers

*and*

# The Croquet Player

# BY THE SAME AUTHOR
## ALL PUBLISHED BY HOUSE OF STRATUS

**FICTION**

ANN VERONICA
APROPOS OF DOLORES
THE AUTOCRACY OF MR PARHAM
BABES IN THE DARKLING WOOD
BEALBY
BRYNHILD
THE BULPINGTON OF BLUP
THE DREAM
THE FIRST MEN IN THE MOON
THE FOOD OF THE GODS
THE HISTORY OF MR POLLY
THE HOLY TERROR
IN THE DAYS OF THE COMET
THE INVISIBLE MAN
THE ISLAND OF DR MOREAU
KIPPS: THE STORY OF A SIMPLE
    SOUL
LOVE AND MR LEWISHAM
MARRIAGE
MEANWHILE
MEN LIKE GODS
A MODERN UTOPIA
MR BRITLING SEES IT THROUGH
THE NEW MACHIAVELLI
THE PASSIONATE FRIENDS
THE SEA LADY
THE SHAPE OF THINGS TO COME
THE TIME MACHINE
TONO-BUNGAY
THE UNDYING FIRE

THE WAR IN THE AIR
THE WAR OF THE WORLDS
THE WHEELS OF CHANCE
WHEN THE SLEEPER WAKES
THE WIFE OF SIR ISAAC HARMAN
THE WONDERFUL VISIT
THE WORLD OF WILLIAM CLISSOLD
    VOLUMES 1,2,3

**NON-FICTION**

THE CONQUEST OF TIME *AND*
    THE HAPPY TURNING
EXPERIMENT IN AUTOBIOGRAPHY
    VOLUMES 1,2
H G WELLS IN LOVE
THE OPEN CONSPIRACY AND OTHER
    WRITINGS

# The Brothers

*and*

# The Croquet Player

# H G WELLS

HOUSE OF
STRATUS

This edition published in 2002 by House of Stratus, an imprint of
House of Stratus Ltd, Thirsk Industrial Park, York Road, Thirsk,
North Yorkshire, YO7 3BX, UK.
Also at: House of Stratus Inc., 2 Neptune Road, Poughkeepsie, NY 12601, USA.

www.houseofstratus.com

Typeset, printed and bound by House of Stratus.

A catalogue record for this book is available from the British Library
and The Library of Congress.

ISBN 0-7551-0394-7

# THE BROTHERS

## CONTENTS

# THE CROQUET PLAYER
## CONTENTS

# The Brothers

To my Friend
J F Horrabin

# CHAPTER ONE

## Important Capture

The immense beauty of the starry night seemed lost upon the man at the window. His attention was concentrated on the gap in the black hills far below him and far away, where a quivering blood-red glow marked the burning suburbs and gardens of the beleaguered city. The smoke flickered still with gun-flashes and the crepitation of the rifle-fire rose and fell and never ceased altogether. Every now and then a momentary incandescence intimated a fresh extension of the conflagration. But the big guns had desisted. Gammet's attack had been held. Gammet was done for.

"High time too," thought the man at the window. "And when Gammet has been cleaned up then *I* will take the city."

Richard Bolaris got up and began pacing the dim room. It was a large, fairly proportioned room and it was lit only by a couple of candles in silver candlesticks on the gigantic writing-desk. Otherwise the whole place was in darkness because of the possibility of an air-raid from the Reds. The huge vulgar furnishings of Orpedimento, the great wine merchant, the nominal owner of this château which Bolaris had requisitioned, achieved a sombre dignity in the obscurity.

1

Bolaris was the latest and newest of strong men; he and the Reds under Ratzel had torn their vague-minded countrymen into two warring swarms, and slowly he was winning his way to an unqualified dictatorship. He had been waiting impatiently for this final opportunity. Gammet had been the chief piece in the King's defence and the piece was now practically lost. Bolaris knew exactly how to behave and what to do next day. The trusty Handon should see to all the details. Gammet had asked for this offensive, staked everything upon it. Bolaris had acted doubt, argued cunningly and bowed at last as if in submission to Gammet and the King. Now he would strike. He would face nothing but a clutch of disgruntled men. "You have thrown away the fourth army," he would say. "Incapacity in itself is a crime, but this is more than incapacity; it is sabotage as I shall prove – treason unashamed."

Handon would have seen to it that the guards were all right, and the morning after when that poor disingenuous royal fool asked after Gammet, he would find that Gammet was shot already, and that there was nothing under his feet or above his head or to the right of him or to the left of him, or before him or behind him in the whole world but the power of Richard Bolaris. And, after his quality, he would pretend to be grateful for the vigilance of Bolaris. And he would bide his time. He was a great man for biding his time was the King.

Physically Bolaris was not a tall man, but he was broad-shouldered and his head was a fine one, a wide forehead above clear hazel eyes and a slightly impish clean-shaven face. His nose was short but well-modelled; his mouth and chin finely made and free of any suggestion of the strong man's jowl. He wore an open-necked shirt and a belt about his civilian trousers, but he kept the men about him up to the mark in their uniforms.

He rehearsed the projected scene and tried a variation or so. Then he dismissed the matter from his mind, touched a stud on the desk and returned slowly to his seat at the open window. He could rest for a time until the reports from the front came in.

A door far up the room opened and the secretary on duty appeared on the threshold between two sentinels. "I'll take anything that is not extremely urgent in the map room in about an hour," said Bolaris, and the bright vertical oblong of the door thinned out and vanished.

"Ah!" said the dictator in the tone of a man who feels his task accomplished. He shook his finger towards the long slopes that hid the city. "I give you a fortnight more, Ratzel. And after that we will have the Corporate State here too – and here, mind you, that will be – whatever I want it to be."

2

Power and more Power. The King unfortunately would have to remain. That went without saying. But side by side with the crown there must be a new title. Why not take a leaf from history and try the Lord Protector? Or something new? The Master Citizen?

And Catherine Farness? She had always been loyal – and sometimes very wise. Bolaris was no egotist. He could admit good advice when he got it. Was she always to remain in the background? Was the Master Citizen always to hide his woman in this shamefaced manner from the world?

Patience. That too he would manage.

The gentle trill of a telephone roused him from his reverie.

"Yes?"

He knew Catherine's inimitable voice even before she said, "It's your Black Cat speaking. With nothing very important to say."

"What is it?"

"Just something silly. Just something I can't say in common words. Something very sentimental. Have you forgotten Lampobo?"

Lampobo was a little language they had invented six years ago when they were lovers in exile in Lugano, to hide their nationality and puzzle observant people in their hotel.

"If anyone listens in to our love talks," he replied, "they have the best chance in the world of standing against a wall." And then rather haltingly in that half-forgotten lingo, he added, "Yes. You see I remember – I don't forget things about *you*."

"Don't flirt," said she. "It isn't that. Something *very* important – "

"What is it?"

"Ratzel has been taken prisoner."

Bolaris whistled softly. That was a queer turn of events. "How?" he asked.

"No particulars. Number Four wants you to know. Number Four knows but other people don't. Knows who it is, I mean. The men who took him don't know. Listen hard. Don't ask me questions. Number Four came to me and asked me to to tell you. Afraid direct to you would be tapped. Said you ought to know before anyone else."

"Good old Handon," whispered Bolaris to himself.

Then to the telephone and dropping the little language, "Where are you, darling?"

"In the little house beyond the hospital."

"I've eaten nothing today practically. Could you give me a supper? Things have gone very badly today and I need consoling." And dropping back into Lampobo, "Number Four and the prisoner too."

"All your desires shall be satisfied," said the lady with a coy laugh that sounded quite natural. "Darling."

Bolaris replaced the telephone and went towards the door clapping his hands loudly. It opened and two sentinels stood at attention and then the young secretary appeared. "I'll take the reports in the map room," said Bolaris. "Is the intelligence officer there? Afterwards I'll go to the fourth hospital for a surprise visit. Have the three cars ready, the pilot car, the armoured car and the whippet with the gun. And then – "

He seemed to consider. "I'll ask Madame Farness to give me supper. She's close by. Will you tell her? You know her telephone number. And telephone me there if I have gone on from the hospital."

The secretary tried not to look too understanding. It would be quite unnecessary he knew to telephone to the hospital.

Bolaris entered the map room with an elation he did his best to control. "None too good, I'm afraid," he said to the intelligence officer. "Tell me what you know. I was against it all from the beginning but the King overruled me. God grant there's been no serious loss of men or material. I hope not. It seemed to me the attack petered out. Do you know what it is burning down there?"

3

The three cars using no lights travelled slowly down through the dark woods below the château, and more swiftly over the flank of the mountain, above the darkened encampments of the Black Legion and the old ninth regiment. In the open the road became more plainly visible as a faint streak on the grey starlit ground. Ever and again there was a challenge, a halt and the scrutiny of an electric torch. They passed through a silent and deserted village and between a mile-long row of still, dark poplars, until the white walls of the old convent turned hospital were reached. There was no pretence of calling there. Bolaris, with his cars and escort, passed straight on through the gates of the little villa beyond and descended at the entrance.

Two sentinels appeared from the shadow of the portico and saluted.

A tall dark woman in a white dress appeared in the doorway.

It was in the spirit of the night that he should speak in an undertone. "They are here?" he asked.

"Both," she said. "The prisoner under guard downstairs."

He followed her into a room lit by a single paraffin lamp. There were provisions on the table and plates and knives, and in the corner stood Handon, in a khaki uniform, a stout figure with an open ruddy face, who saluted his master as though it was a pleasure to do so.

"Tell me about it," said Bolaris.

Each of his interlocutors looked at the other to begin.

"You ought to see him," said the woman.

"You certainly ought to see him," echoed Handon.

They seemed preoccupied with some idea beyond the facts he knew.

"How was he taken? When?"

"Early this morning. They blundered into the Black Legion."

"They?"

"He was with some officers. If you can call them officers. Commissars perhaps. They just rode into our scouts."

"You saw it?"

"Yes. I suppose they were planning some scheme for swinging round on our left, through that gorge that runs towards the river. They didn't know how far our front extended. Our fellows were coming down the gorge and these Reds came out on the bank, not twenty yards away. They wheeled about and he lost control of his horse. He seemed to be a damned poor rider."

Handon stopped short, shocked at himself.

"Not the only one in this war," said Bolaris, with a grin. "Don't apologize."

"He got on the edge of the bank and his horse slipped down it, rolled right down, horse and man, and our chaps were on him in a moment. We could see he was important at once from the way the others came back for him. No good. It was a hundred to one. They vanished over the bank and were a quarter of a mile off before any of our men could scramble up for a shot at them."

"And it's Ratzel?"

"It's surely Ratzel. You know there's always been a story he was like you. He's *extraordinarily* like you."

Bolaris turned to the woman.

"He's *extraordinarily* like you," she confirmed.

7

"It's fantastic. I ought to know. When they brought him here first, I thought it was some mystification of yours. I tried him with Lampobo. Yes. He's as like as *that*."

"If I don't eat I shall drop," said Bolaris and poured himself a glass of wine. All three sat down about the table and Catherine played hostess to the two men. "He is as like as *that*," Bolaris repeated with his mouth full of chicken. "It gives me a sort of fellow feeling for him. Maybe we'll have to shoot him. He's the backbone of this defence. It will knock the stuffing out of them. All the same if he's hungry…

"Let's have him up. A man talks all the easier for a few glasses of wine. I've never believed in those third degree methods of yours, Handon. Bring him up and stand him there at the end of the table with two of your men behind him. And two at the door. Window all right? Put a man outside there. Light some candles over there and there. It wouldn't do for Catherine's lamp to go out suddenly and leave us in the dark. They say he's a resourceful devil. And if I think proper I'll ask him to supper."

His quick eyes ran round the room. "That's all right," he confirmed. "Yes."

# CHAPTER TWO

## The Prisoner

Their resemblance had certainly not been exaggerated. Ratzel came in with a look of resolute resistance on his face, which changed to blank astonishment as he looked at Bolaris. He was wearing an open red shirt, that differed only from his captor's in its colour. His hair was longer; he was disarmed and his hands were tied. He was the first to speak. "I'll be damned!" he exclaimed.

"Shot first, you'll be," said Bolaris. "What do you mean by looking so infernally like me?"

"I might ask the same question."

"It's my place to ask questions."

"Coincidence. Can we by any chance be related?"

"I say *I* ask the questions. What is your name?"

"Robert Ratzel."

"Age?"

"Thirty-four."

"Place of birth?"

"Hulkingtown, Missouri."

Bolaris became silent.

"We are related," said Ratzel suddenly.

9

"No! Speak when you are spoken to."

"But we *are*. I begin to realize – "

"Tell him not to talk," said Bolaris to the man beside the prisoner. The guard made a prompt movement.

"*I* won't talk," Ratzel volunteered.

An awkward silence descended upon the room. Everyone was looking very intently at Bolaris.

"I am a native-born citizen of this country," he said as if addressing a considerable audience. "I have never been in the United States of America. Never. I cannot even speak English, while the prisoner, as you will note, speaks our language with a marked English accent. Yes. Yes. An American accent. It's very similar. Well, I have stopped him on the verge of claiming kinship with me on the strength of our certainly very remarkable resemblance. Our superficial resemblance. I can quite understand his motives... It will do him no good if he does."

Ratzel seemed about to speak but Bolaris held up a hand to silence him, a gesture reinforced by the guard, who gripped the prisoner's wrists. "Let go," said Bolaris. "I trust his discretion."

He reflected on his course of action.

"It looks to me," he said, "as though you could do with a little food and drink. I myself want to go on eating. I will put you on your parole, eh? And you will join us? I mean you will join our meal."

Ratzel nodded.

"Release his hands. Sit down, sir."

Catherine filled a plate with chicken, white nut and pimento, and handed it to one of the guards to put before her guest.

There was a prolonged pause in the conversation. The men ate. The lady was smilingly but silently hospitable. Bolaris seemed to be considering his next move. When it came, it had an amazing quality of irrelevance.

"I wonder," he said, "if this country is ever likely to produce a literature comparable to any of the great European literatures. What do you think, Ratzel? Or don't you take an interest in that sort of thing?"

Ratzel stopped short with an attractive mouthful on his fork. He replaced it on his plate. After staring for a moment at his captor, he glanced at Catherine, who was watching him with a faint smile in her eyes. His expression of surprise gave place to one of bright response. "If that's your game," he seemed to decide, "I can play it."

"A lot of European literature", he began, in a voice and with a manner that sounded almost like a parody of Bolaris, "is very much overrated. In fact almost all literature is overrated – in comparison with what is possible. Hitherto literature has been essentially aristocratic or bourgeois. It has been written mainly for people who wanted to feel secure, to please and reassure them. It has been leisure reading. Bric-à-brac. Tapestry. Stylistic or gentlemanly sham-careless. The English Jane Austen is quite typical. Quintessential I should call her. A certain ineluctable faded charm. Like some of the loveliest butterflies – with no guts at all. But here and now, we are tearing up life by the roots and anything we write – when we get to writing again – will be fundamental – vital, black, red, vibrating…"

The speaker resumed his interrupted meal.

The two listeners at the table heard this cultured speech with ill-concealed astonishment. They looked at the speaker, they looked at Bolaris and remarked the similarity of the smile upon the two confronted faces. Then Catherine glanced at the guards for any gleam of comprehension. But the guards, who manifestly did not understand a word of it all, had assumed expressions of disciplined dignity.

"When we have settled up with your atrocious attempt to assist in carrying the world back to the dark ages," Ratzel resumed. He took a large mouthful. "Our boys will write. I think they will write well."

"If we let them," said Bolaris.

"This is the seventh grand attack you have made. Tell me about it."

"I shall be in the city in a fortnight."

"I knew it would fail."

"You didn't, I gather, see very much of it."

"No. But I knew your foreign friends with the tanks wouldn't like the idea of coming through those open fields in the centre when they realized we had irrigated them carefully every night. There'd be I felt – well – indecision... Did we capture most of those tanks or did the funk begin before they had come on far enough? Did we get most or only just some?"

"The attack was none of my planning," said Bolaris.

"Many?"

The question went unanswered.

"Why you had your Black Legion up in the air out of the game on our right I can't imagine! It might as well have been bathing at the seaside for all the good it was."

"Anyhow it got you."

"You got *me*. How could a sane man have expected them out there? But it does not matter. I shall hardly be missed. No man is indispensable in a popular mass defence. The enthusiasm in the city is invincible. You can hardly imagine it."

"I don't imagine it. I know all about it. Their discipline is atrocious."

"They don't loot," said Ratzel.

"They kill priests."

"Each side kills priests nowadays. When they get in the way, and they do get in the way."

Bolaris went off at a tangent again. "What has happened to the Royal Galleries? There were some very beautiful things in them."

"Your imported bombers were careless and ignorant. But most of the best things are well taken care of. Do you know the Galleries at all? There was a long narrow gallery of late Italian and French heroic stuff. The art director – and how I agree with him! – left that to the last, and one of those new incendiary bombs they have sent you now, got it. I have always disliked that sort of painting myself, Rapes of the Sabines, the Looting of Corinth and all that stuff. Always reminded me of turning out linen for the laundry – sprawling naked women instead of nice ordinary soiled linen. We all have our likes and dislikes."

He returned to his plate with the air of a man who does not wish to monopolize a conversation.

"I know very little about pictures," said Bolaris modestly, and proceeded to disprove the statement by a dissertation on painting that would have been a model for an English University extension lecture or any small all-about-art-in-half-an-hour handbook (q.v.). Occasionally the prisoner interjected an intelligent remark, but for the most part he nodded and ate.

13

Then abruptly Bolaris came to an end. He consulted a wrist watch and signalled to the two guards, who came to attention. Ratzel finished his wine appreciatively and stood up.

## 2

Bolaris lifted his glass to his departing guest. "I am sorry you have to return to your quarters downstairs. They are far from perfect – but civil war is always uncivilized. A class war more particularly so. No chivalry. Later on maybe I may have to shoot you. But I do hope that before then we may have a chance to resume what I have found a very agreeable conversation indeed. War would be intolerable without such occasional interludes…"

The prisoner was led out.

Directly the door had closed upon him Bolaris' manner changed. "Get outside," he said to the remaining guards, and Catherine and Handon shifted closer to him because they felt that what he had to say would not be said too loudly. Catherine's expression was one of anticipatory appreciation; Handon's intimated a hopeless curiosity struggling against complete stupefaction.

"*Now*," said Bolaris. "You have been a little puzzled by – what shall I call it? – the untimely refinement – the cultured irrelevance of our conversation. But I had to talk about something – or rather I had to talk about nothing. I wanted to look at him. I wanted to look him over. And I didn't want him to talk to me. I wanted to draw out our resemblances and differences. I wanted to note any distinctive mannerisms he had – for a good reason. I wanted time to think about what to do next – with him in front of me. And the curious thing is that he came more than half-way to meet me. He took my point very quickly. He was quite ready to play the man of culture, reluctantly at war. Just as I might have done. I couldn't catch him saying anything or moving in any way that was distinctive between us. Could you? I'd heard we have a resemblance. But this is a Double."

"It is incredible that – " Catherine was beginning, and then she caught a warning glance in his eyes. "What do you think of it, Handon?" she asked.

"I don't like him," said Handon compactly. "I disagree."

"One thing I noted," said Catherine. "His accent *is* American."

"And I?"

"You have no accent. Why should you have?"

"You don't like him, Handon?"

"He's sinister."

"But my double?"

"He *looks* like you," said Handon, and paused before he added, "but, mind you – he isn't you."

"Yes," said Bolaris slowly, with an air of receiving a very important statement. "I think that is – probably – correct."

"He is completely different," said Handon. "I can see through him."

"And you see?"

"A Red. Everything we are fighting against. Everything you stand against."

"That may well be," said Bolaris deliberately, "all the same there is something about him, some possibility, some opportunity. It is well you sent for me as you did. Your instincts, Handon, are always sound. I feel – what do I feel? Handon, I feel that I haven't got it – and yet that it's just at my fingers' ends. If

15

he is like me, I am like him. That opens – possibilities. For example – away there, nineteen miles as the crow flies, like all the secrets of the defence."

"But what do you mean?"

"To talk to those fellows! To see it from *their* side! That would be something."

"You mustn't dream of impersonating him!" cried Handon. "If you leave us – even for a day – "

"*You* would carry on. I could trust the Five."

"But if something *new* arose? And if they spotted it and *got* you? *They* wouldn't hesitate to shoot. Think how they shot Mand. And with everything – as things are."

"I'm not going to do it. But I want to turn all these possibilities over in my mind. You must trust me to do that. I want to see him some more – worm things out of him… Anyhow I want to stay here… And all the time things are happening at the château."

He lowered his voice.

"There is a particular thing, Handon, I want said to the representative of a certain foreign power about those new tanks. I'm a little doubtful about that slim youngster, the new assistant secretary. I want it brought home to our friends that if they *will* insist on keeping their own men in those tanks – who don't know the language, who can't question a peasant, who can't find their way about, who don't care a damn for our cause, they are bound to keep bunched up, and if they bunch up they can be laid for. As they were today. Very gently but very firmly I want that said. Between ourselves it wasn't really Gammet's fault. So far as the loss of the tanks goes. But that's another question. Until *our* men are in those tanks, Handon, the confounded contraptions are part of a potential army of occupation. The King would as soon be nursed by a foreign army – as nursed by – us. I want someone who has this in mind to be at the château when our good friends ring through. And at the same time I've got this sense of something immensely important here. I want to be here."

"I could go back," said Handon.

"Take the cars and send them back for me."

"But I don't like leaving you."

"I know. When you're not about nowadays, Handon, it's like leaving one's right hand upstairs."

"You'll do nothing rash with that fellow?"

"*Really*, Handon!"

"Forgive a loyal anxiety. In my instincts, in my bones I distrust him."

"I stretch out my right hand where it is most needed."

Bolaris got up and, clapping his hand affectionately upon his adherent's shoulder-blades, steered him towards the door.

3

Bolaris and Catherine stood at the small window beside the portico of the villa and watched the cars pause for a moment to check with the sentinels and then vanish one after the other through the gates. Bolaris laid his hand on Catherine's further shoulder and drew her face towards his own, a familiarity he would never have allowed himself in the jealous presence of Handon.

"That gets rid of *him*," he said.

She let her cheek touch his ever so lightly.

But Bolaris, she perceived, was not in the mood for making love that night. He was thinking of Handon. "Handon," he said, "is the perfect lieutenant, the ideal disciple, the loyalest of the Five."

She thought for a moment. "You make people like that."

"I never made Handon. He was born, not made… Darling, when at last we are in the city and the whole country is ours, and I have settled certain little affairs of which you know, then, I suppose, you think, as everybody thinks, that I shall be dictator, a real dictator, and do just exactly as I like."

She was quick to take his meaning. "There will be Handon, of course," she said.

"There will be Handon," he said softly. "There will be all the Five. There will be the Bands, the Inner Circle, the Boys. There will be all that I have said, because I wanted to hear how it sounded and all that I said because I knew it would win them. And all that I have been to them and all that I am to them. A man fettered from head to foot in what is expected of him. His own slave. I shall have to do what is expected of me at every turn. As much a sacrifice as one of those magic kings you read about in Frazer's *Golden Bough*… Catherine, dear, the other night I had a dream. It was a triumph. I was on the balcony of the palace above the great square over there, and they were cheering me and cheering me. Silver trumpets. Banners. Waving flags. Crowds as far as the eye could reach. And a sort of horror of myself came upon me. I found I was not moving myself. I was being moved. My nerves had become wires. I was made to lift up my hand and salute the crowd. I was caught. I was frozen. I had become an automaton… And then quite suddenly I was alone with you. I was weeping, my dear; I was kneeling at your feet between your knees and weeping in your arms. As I did – you remember that time? I was doing it because that is what I felt like doing and not what I had to do. And then – outside – the cheering had changed to howling."

She kissed him very softly.

"And now," he said, abruptly withdrawing his arm, "for my brother."

"Your brother?" she cried.

"Obviously my brother."

"But *how*, your brother?"

"I don't know. *He* does. I want him to tell me."

"Your *brother!*"

"Worse than that. Dearest! – my *Twin*. No one must know, of course. We must hush it up. No dictatorship could stand it for a moment. Think of Handon! Oh my dear! think of Handon!"

Bolaris was seized by laughter. The sentinels outside heard him and exchanged glances of amazement. She loved his swift changes to laughter and her heart within her laughed. For he had scarcely laughed at all since his first repulse before the city. He had been dark and moody.

"Handon's whole soul is fighting against it now! The devotee, the fanatic, the soul of loyalty! The psychological struggle going on in that car up the hill must be stupendous. Twins! It is something he will *not* believe – cannot believe. Not even half-brothers. Not even mere brothers. Never will that frightful realization get into his head – unless it is driven in with a nail and hammer. The obvious was already fighting for life in him – and losing, when he talked just now. How could he, how could anyone of his quality be devoted to a *Twin*? *You*, my dear, were slightly shaken. Oh yes! you were. There was a faint recoil. Don't I

19

know? *You'll* get over it. But for him! Two of me! And one of them on the other side! It would give his poor wits a sort of permanent squint. From the very moment he set eyes on Ratzel he realized that such a being was intolerable. Impossible. Ratzel, he feels, is sheer blasphemy. Taking my likeness in vain. A revolting caricature... If Handon can contrive to kill him he will. Mark my words. Shoot him and bury him and forget about him. Or rather not forget about him, but go on to a story that in no respect was it possible to mistake him for me. Ratzel will become shorter – very, very, *very* ugly – sinister..."

He clapped his hands for an officer. "Bring the prisoner to me in the room upstairs. I want to question him in private."

# CHAPTER THREE

## Twin-Destinies

A s soon as the guards who had brought up Ratzel had taken their places outside the door, Bolaris left the window from which he had been watching the glare of the distant conflagration as it fluctuated between the black silhouette of the motionless agaves, and came and sat on the settee beside his prisoner. Catherine Farness stood questioningly, unsure whether her presence was wanted.

"Come and sit by us," said Bolaris, putting a chair for her. "This maybe is one of those matters where your wits are better than mine. Look at him! Can you doubt he is my twin brother?"

"But I thought you denied – " began Ratzel.

"I did. I had to. For reasons of state. I lied. I hate lying – it's the dry rot of politics. But you were on the point of saying too much. I had to shut you up at once. I said I was never in the United States of America. Well, I *was* in the United States. *My* story begins as a foundling in New Orleans thirty-two years ago. My age was guessed at as about one year ten months old."

"Thirty-four. Then that clinches it all. I *had* a twin brother."

"That was what I didn't want you to blurt out."

"Exactly. I understand perfectly. I *had* a twin brother. I have one now, I realize. My long-lost twin brother. It's melodramatic. We ought to burst into a duet about it. Thirty-two years ago was the great flood year. Gods, what floods they must have been! It was the ruination of a whole country. The waters rose so suddenly at Hulkingtown that our mother couldn't get back to the house — she had waded and clambered out to the store. I suppose you and I were left in different beds or in different rooms. Anyhow the man who carried me out — he had to jump for the boat when the house collapsed — thought I was the only kid in the shack. My mother told me about it a hundred times. It was always on her mind. How she got to the embankment above the house and how she stood screaming against the wind and the rain, "Two of them! *Two!*" Nobody heard her. It was three days before she could find where I was and claim me. You and the house went swirling off. Heaven knows how *you* weren't drowned. The shack was surely smashed somewhere near down the river. Did you get in a box? Did you get into a cupboard or something?"

"I haven't the faintest idea. It was only when I was seventeen or eighteen, as a result of a violent quarrel between my foster father and his second wife, that I learnt I was a foster child. I remember nothing of America. Nothing. I grew up here. I doubt if I know three hundred words of English. I had always supposed I was the actual son of General Bolaris. He and his wife were in New Orleans at the time of the floods; they were coming home from South America, they had thought of adopting a child, and they adopted me. What happened to you?"

"You got a bourgeois education."

"I had a good education. I went to the University here."

22

He nodded casually towards those far-away flickerings.

"I had a time in the Military Academy and then I tried journalism and politics."

"Life wasn't as easy as that for me," said Ratzel.

"Tell me about your mother," said Catherine Farness.

"*His* mother too," said Ratzel smiling. "She was, as people say, the best of mothers. But she really was the best of mothers. Rather big, blonde, plucky, excitable, devoted. And no luck. She died when I was twelve years old."

"Odd! *My* mother died when I was twelve years old," said Bolaris. "Or rather my foster mother. It's a little difficult to adjust all at once to the new situation. For all those years she was in effect a very real mother to me. What was our father like?"

"I never knew him. He was engineer on a river steamboat and he was drowned before I can remember much about him. My mother had a hard time, scraping a living down there in the south. She tried to get me educated. First in Louisiana and then in Georgia. Not so easy. Poor whites is what they called our sort. I was precocious. I tried to get north. Not so easy for a sweated worker. They won't let you go. Never mind about those early struggles. I knew pretty bitterly what it was to be a proletarian before I was fifteen. Then I had luck – I broke my leg and was put into Glegges Hospital down at Red River and I got away from there."

"You broke your leg when you were fifteen?" said Bolaris. "*I* broke my leg when I was fifteen. I'm beginning to believe in horoscopes. We were born under the same stars."

"Roughly maybe. I'm not superstitious. I've noted in a lot of things that Coincidence seems to be carrying on an everlasting guerrilla war against Probability – but it never amounts to anything practical, Anyhow, the more *you* believe in horoscopes the better for me. You won't be in such a hurry to put me up against a wall and finish me."

"There will be a strong disposition on the part of my associates to put you up against a wall anyhow, as soon as they know who you are."

"I understand that."

"You can't let that happen," said Catherine Farness to Bolaris.

"You don't frighten me with an imaginary horoscope," said Bolaris. "If he's truly my brother he'll quite understand if he has to be shot and behave like a gentleman. But we aren't talking about putting against walls just now. What happened in that hospital?"

"I got hold of books. I was always a glutton for books. But the point is that it was possible to get away north from there. Then indeed I read."

"*I* was reading when I was fifteen, sixteen, seventeen. Fermenting with ideas. I was a bit of a socialist for a time. It's wonderful what a boy does in those years. Learns a universe."

"He learns a universe," said Ratzel. "And judges it."

"A bit prematurely?"

"When you start as a southern town factory worker, you soon get the gist of the evidence," said Ratzel.

"*Against*," said Bolaris.

Ratzel considered that for a moment. "Possibly there is something in that," he said.

Catherine Farness was an alert intelligence glowing between them and she brightened at his concession.

And now they began a talk. But no book can do justice to a talk about ideas if it gives what is said verbatim. They talked with the quick sensitiveness of their common nature, but also they beat about the bush and harked backwards and forwards. Sometimes they lost touch and had some trouble to recover it. And for the sake of the reader the story-teller must give a foreshortened account of what they said – an arranged talk, all point and gist.

2

"Why are you a communist, Ratzel?" said Bolaris.

"Why did you drop your college socialism? And go over to the Right? You – with our brains."

"Why did you come here? I was adopted and brought – but what brought you?"

"I came with a batch of miners fifteen years ago – to open up the Gorram Mines and show your people how. We got high pay. Even by American rates. They might have got Poles or Belgians, but they preferred us. In the long run they reckoned we should give less trouble. We were picked over – hundred per cent Americans – guaranteed free from all revolutionary ideas – with an inborn hatred in fact of Radicals and Reds. So they thought."

"Their mistake."

"In a way. Fifteen years ago that was. In those days the words communism or socialism didn't cut much ice in America. We thought Revolution was a game for Wops and Dagoes. Why! in those days we despised the English workers for being on the dole. Funny to think of that now. We Americans, I realize, more and more, are the most lawless and revolutionary people on earth – but we don't like to give it a name. In our bones we know we are really a new people – and it frightens us. Americans will sail at

25

top speed towards socialism without a qualm – unless you wave a red flag at them…"

"Maybe it's all the better if they call American realities by American names," said Bolaris. "Your Red jargon, dictatorship of the proletariat, proletariat, bourgeoisie and so on and so forth, is about as sloppy a lingo, forgive me, as the human mind ever slipped up upon. Not a classification in it that is sound, not a term that isn't like a thin paper bag full of broken eggs… Dogmas made by exasperated refugees with chronic indigestion."

"I rather agree with you," said Ratzel, tranquilly. "I've had to listen to so much more of it than you have. But after a while you don't listen any more to the words and phrases because you hear something behind the words and phrases. Something absolutely real. An indignation."

Catherine spoke. "*We* hate fighting that."

Ratzel looked at her. "You've talked of it already?"

"In a way. Sometimes we hardly need to talk."

"*We* are like that," said Ratzel.

"Don't say I have a double also?"

"No," considered Ratzel. "But there is a sort of parallel."

"Go on with what you were saying," said Catherine. "That is more important."

"Yes," said Bolaris, "it *is* more important… That indignation… Human indignation. It's an essential word."

He was evidently trying to get something clear in his mind. The two others waited for him to speak.

"You see," said Bolaris; "there is an indignation on our side."

"Rather like the indignation of a fat dog with a big bone who is sniffed at by an impertinent starving mongrel."

"Not altogether that. No. He got the bone for himself anyhow and there's a whole pack of the mongrels. For all that, brother Ratzel, our two indignations may not be so very different in essence as you seem to think."

"Against stupid acquisitiveness, careless cruelty?"

"Well – what of stupid resentment, stupid vindictiveness?... Never mind that for the present. There's one or two things between us more important than recrimination. You say that I seem to think this and that. That's interesting. *Think*, you say. When do you imagine I think nowadays? It comes to me like a blow that I don't think any more. So far as I know I've done no thinking – I've done nothing but scheming – for the past two years. Politics, management, war, the next immediate thing and then the next immediate thing. Years ago perhaps I thought. And suddenly I'm thinking again now."

"Yes. It's been much the same with me. We've been so busy..."

"Until this remarkable fact that we two people, who may be almost identically alike inside, find ourselves here in the most direct antagonism... That sets us thinking again in spite of ourselves... We've just carried on. But am I thinking now? I ask you. Good Heavens! My head's spinning faster and faster. And yet not fast enough for me. I want to talk this out with you and nothing will wait for us to talk. Have you ever thought, Ratzel, how the poor human mind is being left behind nowadays by the rush of events? Not only us. 'Do something,' they say to us, and 'Tell us what to do! Decide! Decide!' If only these damned scientific men would invent something – a mental accelerator that would make us think fifty times as fast as we do now – and not get fatigued, not get raw and bitter, then we might do

27

something with the world. Well, let us say what we can in the time we have. In an hour and a half at latest I must start back for – up there…

"Now about this indignation of yours – let's get it clear. I began life with much the same indignation. I insist – the same indignation. Remember, I told you, I was a socialist as a student. Do you think I didn't perceive that the mass of humanity was being used up to no good purpose and wasted? What does your indignation amount to? What *is* it really? The first thing I want to ask you is this: Have you ever tried to estimate the personal element in indignation? How far your indignation at your own experience gives it force and substance?"

He paused. Ratzel smiled. When he spoke he spoke more deliberately than his brother. He was more exact and less nimble. He spoke like one accustomed to be heard attentively and in-terpreted and misinterpreted by sincere and jealously dogmatic men and women, while Bolaris spoke like a man used to inattentive listeners.

"What you suggest is perfectly sound," Ratzel admitted. "*My* indignation was never disinterested. No. Never. I was indignant primarily because I found myself attacked, threatened with subjugation and obliged to struggle. It was the amazement and wrath of a child when first it is crossed. I began with tremendous expectations – as all young creatures do. And I discovered I belonged to a frustrated class before I was fourteen. I had been given life and I had been cheated of life. My promised world, the beautiful toy ball they taught me about, had been stolen from me almost as soon as it had been put into my hands. I was, I realized, condemned to live in need and humiliation, toiling, wanting, caught in that vile township with not one chance in a hundred thousand of escape. Everyone about me, everyone of my sort, seemed to be in much the same plight. So I looked round to find who had stolen my world."

"Wait a minute," said Bolaris. "I know what you concluded had stolen your world, the damned bourgeoisie and all that. Maybe you think it still. But let me ask – myself as well as you – a more essential question. Isn't it possible that this indignation of ours is something deeper in the nature of life than either you or I have supposed? Isn't it in the nature of young life to expect – extremely? To set out to conquer the world? Isn't all new life *eager*? Isn't all life indignant and fighting? Is any vital activity anything much more than an indignant struggle? I – I was indignant just as much as you were. Not quite in the same way. Though not as you say a mere mean indignation – the dog with the bone and all that. I didn't feel robbed perhaps but I felt hampered and encumbered. The toy ball wasn't so much snatched from me as punctured, until it shrank to something crumpled and unsatisfactory. I was only to play with it in a certain way – a stupid way. I had liberties on conditions. Mean conditions. It wasn't good enough."

Catherine nodded with the expression of one who sees the solution of a long-pondered riddle plain before her.

"Let me tell my story now that I have begun it," said Ratzel. "I saw the Capitalist System plain, as the world thief. I saw life as a choice between world revolution or life-long slavery. It seemed to me that everyone except the robbers *must* see things like that. The masses would arise, once you opened their eyes, wrench back the world from its exploiters – "

"And all would be well?" said Bolaris.

29

"All would be well. I gave myself to the World Revolution before I was eighteen."

"And now?"

"I have given myself to this idea of a World Revolution. The thing is done. Here I am."

"But because you wanted to fulfil yourself," said Bolaris. "You saw frustration in economic slavery. I saw frustration from a different angle. I didn't believe, I don't believe, in the power of these indignant masses of yours to take over and manage affairs. I didn't believe in that solidarity your side is always assuming; your proletariat seemed to me to be just as credulous, stupid, impulsive, incalculable as rich people. More even. I couldn't persuade myself to your mystical belief in mass direction. Were *you* really persuaded about that? Didn't you perhaps jump rather hastily to an easy conclusion?"

"And how did you jump?"

"To another easy conclusion maybe. But not that one. Since you lived mostly with people who were driven from above, obliged to work and obliged to work in particular unpleasant ways and sometimes even deprived of the work that opened the door for them to even the most elementary satisfactions, while you, I say, had all the odds against you, it was easy for you to take refuge in the belief that if your sort were only given half a chance to assert itself and take control of things – Heavens, how different it would be! But I wasn't one of the underdogs. I was one of the released. And I saw and knew what released people could do, and all that in the worst sense they were capable of doing. I was brought up among released people, among people who had an air of controlling things, giving directions – military people, lawyers, priests and teachers, newspaper owners, industrialists, and what hit me was not indignation at oppression but indignation at presumption and pretentious meanness and muddle. You thought these people of the Right, as you would call them, were cruel and hard; I knew they were – fatuous. I saw enough of human incapacity to disbelieve in the ability of any sort of intelligent management of our affairs with the normal badly trained stuff of humanity we have today. A director is a director still and a colonel a colonel, even if you call them commissars. But these people here were uneasy and more aware of their own incapacity than your inexperienced rebels. Less conceit and more cowardice and cunning. They want a Strong Man to make them feel safe. Demand creates supply. I seem to give them what they want. I have a certain aptitude for this silly war business and a reasonable share of political trickiness. Anyhow, said I – and that maybe is where the family vanity comes in, Ratzel – the stronger the grip I get upon affairs the less of their foolery need I suffer. I'm told that away there in the city, your general behaviour has had – a fairly similar flavour."

Ratzel considered. "There has to be a phase – it is fundamental in Communist theory – of trusteeship."

"Your dictatorship of the proletariat, I agree. But God help the trustees! Against themselves. Your trustee in Russia shows more than a hint of moral strain. Eh? But I also have exactly the same idea about myself – of trusteeship, which is roughly that anyone else would be worse. At bottom it is *my* frustration I am fighting against. At bottom it is *my* indignation that drives. I am not trying to interpret or reconcile or implement the forces behind me. I'm trying to make them go what I believe to be the sane way. I'd as soon ask my lot to tell me where to go next as the man with the dog would ask the sheep. Is that anything different from what you are doing? Are you *obeying* this indignation of the proletariat or are you *using* it? What shape or direction is there in it to obey? Tell me, Ratzel, frankly, brother to brother, now that you have seen your particular brand of indignation sweep like a flame about the world, has it done much more than burn up a certain amount of old rubbish, break up a few old traditions and organizations, smash and break and burn like a resentful child in a tantrum who has got hold of the matches? But *make* – ?

"Is it really a new world you and your Communists are making? Anywhere? Moscow? Mexico? North China?"

"Not yet," said Ratzel and then, "but the spirit is there. Hope. The spirit for a new world. We have been so busy fighting you lot. And – there is a complicatedness about things."

"The spirit is everywhere – I have it quite as much as you have – but are your lot over there really giving it an operative form? That's one of my phrases, brother – *operative form*. And another which isn't mine – it came from someone on your side – is *competent receiver*. *Competent receiver* and *operative form*; two phrases for two problems that Socialism and Communism ought to have tackled forty years ago. We know pretty accurately what is going on behind your front. We know about your troubles. All the shooting in the city hasn't been at us. We know how you suffer from the touchy dissentient, the egotist who must assert himself by making difficulties, the disciple who pesters to be persuaded like an amorous woman, the devotee who must never be slighted, the praise-hunters, the asinine 'kicker' who flames into jealousy, who *likes* to flare up and is proud of it, at any hint of leadership. Quite apart from the fools who are downright rascals, fanatics today and rascals tomorrow. We know of their groups and their – what is your word? – deviations. We know of

32

your would-be successors in the city there. Some of them must be getting busy now. But they'll be scared. They want you to win this war for them before they do you down. You all have the same brand of indignation over there, no doubt, just as you have similar heads and feet, you have your proletarian indignation, but it doesn't hold you together in any real co-operation. You're just a crowd of empty *antis* – without a creative idea in common."

"I do my best to discipline the Party," said Ratzel reflectively.

"We know you do," said Bolaris cheerfully. "Lot of fools they are. Don't you want to get up now and then and kick 'em all round *hard*, good and hard, every man Jack of them?"

Ratzel's smile returned to his face. "Tell me about *your* lot."

"Just as impossible. If it wasn't for the civil war and their fear of *your* lot, the whole damned dog team would have me out of the sledge and be at each other's throats tomorrow."

Ratzel smiled at Catherine – and his smile was exactly like what she called Bolaris' old-fashioned look.

"Very similar isn't it. *My* lot holds together because they hate your lot, and your lot holds together because they are afraid of mine. But except that your lot is Anti-Red, I can't tell what they are up to. We do at any rate *talk* of the classless society and so on. We do dream of something generous and fraternal. But you? Are you monarchist, Bolaris, with a pious loyalty to that sly, futile, pin-head of yours, or are you clerical with a mysterious belief in that unbreakable triplex God who crucified Himself to put the Pope in the Vatican, and who prefers Reds to be shot in heaps and children sweated rather than interfere, or are you on the side of those dreary cash registers who run the mines and transport, or the colonels and majors who just want men to order about, or these grandee landlords of yours with a passion for swagger, slavery and sex? Which is it, Bolaris? Think of them. You are too close up to them. You should see them from away there in the city. *What* a lot!"

"It *is* a lot as you say."

"Much worse than yours?" asked Catherine of Ratzel.

"More to blame because they have had opportunities."

"Less to blame because they have had temptations. If you knew some of the heroisms of our men – !"

Catherine seemed to hesitate. "Maybe," she doubted.

"Much the same stuff really," said Bolaris. "Well – I answer you in your own words; I too – I want to discipline my party. I want a humanity chastened and informed and disciplined. *Educated*. Really educated. What we are dealing with, you and I, in ourselves and everyone else is – an untrained, unquickened animal; animal still; a greedy, cowardly animal whose only loyalty is a disguised Narcissism."

"You speak plainly," said Ratzel.

"Because usually I do not have to speak at all. That's my advantage over you."

"No," interrupted Catherine suddenly. "You are going too far, Richard dear. You are too hard on our humanity. May I say something? I have played a woman's part in the world, and that is to look on while things are being done. And learn. The creature is a child – not really a stuck-up monkey but a childish man. It isn't a wicked old *formed* animal, like an old gorilla or a boar or a crocodile. It's a cub. No human being really grows up mentally – *yet*. That is the trouble with men and women. They are all infants mentally, physically precocious. They are as greedy, credulous, vain and heartless as any other young animals. I'm not talking theory; I'm talking biological fact. Yes – I could prove it

34

to you by Axolotl and Amphioxus and gregarious animals and all sorts of established scientific ideas."

"You've been reading biology!" said Bolaris. "What *don't* you read?"

"Women ought to read. A sacred duty. I read biology. I read psychology. I read everything because I want to understand you. You are my job, Richard dear, just as the world is yours. And things like that I am beginning to understand."

"Dear governess!"

"But I think that what you say is absolutely right," said Ratzel turning to Catherine, and Bolaris laid his hand for a moment on Catherine's because when he called her "governess" he had wanted to call her "mother-mistress", and he had been too shy to say so.

"Human beings *are* children," said Ratzel, taking on her idea. And we, except in such gleams of sanity as this – when we get three brains working hard instead of one – are children too. When all is said and done about loyalty to the will of the people and so forth and so on, what we do is to manage them."

He grinned cheerfully. "As some women manage us."

"No. We would if we could," said Catherine. "But all we with our feminine minds can do is to think in terms of individuals, by and through individuals, and it is you who must be responsible for the whole. Whether it's sound and complete or not."

Bolaris and Ratzel nodded agreement.

"Somehow it seems to me that here perhaps we have the two halves of one scheme. But that may be my headlong imagination," said Catherine. "Is that so?"

"What have we got in common?" said Bolaris. "Quite a lot."

"I began by being indignant on my own score no doubt," said Ratzel. "But – at any rate I'm no longer infantile."

"I believe *he* is the nearest thing to a grown man I have ever known," said Catherine. "And you too seem much of an age."

"I am growing up – well and good. I want to see a new world freed from smothered indignation, from the madness that comes out of hopeless discontent. I believe that a new world, a fullness of human life, such as men have never dreamt of before, is possible now. But we have still to learn the way to it. There has to be a new education. An education with steel in it. Exactly what you have said. I want to get my hands on power to bring that about, and so do you. I want to discover and mobilize everyone in the world who can be made like-minded with myself. And I don't care a rap for the others. Not a rap. Naturally I want to revolutionize all this jungle of industrialism that has grown up about us. That is to say I want a real Socialism. I want mankind *drilled* – and I don't care how hard they are drilled – into a proper use of property and money – a proper respect. Respect the work done. Respect the promise which you call wages. And I don't care if I have to hang every speculator in the world."

"I am as ready to alter all that as you are," said Bolaris. "And my hand, mind you, is nearer the necks of the rich than yours."

"I hate greedy incompetence that has to compel and crush because it cannot direct and govern."

"And so do I. I hate indiscipline."

"And so do I."

"I hate that continual congealing of officialism and professionalism and custom, which is like the hardening of arteries in the state."

"*Well!*" said Ratzel, meeting a new idea there. "Yes, so do I... And priests."

"All sane men resent priests," said Bolaris.

"And where do you differ?" asked Catherine.

"We don't differ," said Bolaris. "Evidently when we scrap our catch-words, we don't differ. This isn't a collision, it is a meeting."

"It has been a wonderful meeting," she said. "But the night is passing. Time waits for no man. The cars have been back an hour and are waiting for you, Richard. The children want to go on with their civil war, gratify old grudges, get their revenges, feel important in their uniforms. What is the next phase? Are you going to stop them? What are you two adults going to do?"

3

"Well?" said Ratzel.

"You first, brother. Brother – ?"

"Brother Robert. No, you first. I am corrupted by speaking perpetually to the faithful in their Marxist jargon. I am evasive, redundant, politic. I know it. I tend to gabble away from the question in hand. Think aloud, brother – Brother – ?"

"Brother Richard," said Catherine softly.

"I will. I am virtually dictator now. Gammet is done for. I clean him up tomorrow. The rich people will truckle to me and pay – pay, the King will try to outwit me, with what you call his pin-head, the generals will applaud me but insist I'm too soft with the men and too hard upon jealous officers, the church will bless me publicly and mutter. They hate me like poison, but they believe that I, and I alone, can save them from a reckoning with you Reds. Thank Heaven, they have a tremendous idea of you. They believe there may be a Red Judgment yet. That's the nightmare in which I ride to power. You, you Reds, you poor squabbling Reds, keep me in power. If you are defeated, wiped out – Gods! it will be like hounds upon a fox."

"Our positions," reflected Ratzel, "are extraordinarily parallel."

"We depend on one another. We live and die together. Our horoscopes are left and right of the same picture. Catherine, I cannot help it, we have to keep on with the war."

"Until?"

"Until his power there and mine here have been so consolidated – that we can tell them."

"But what goes on meanwhile? You foster reaction and he a tyranny."

"No. We make nothing really. We foster very little. Perhaps presently we will have a sort of peace, an armed peace, with perpetual snarling and menaces. What is really happening is the birth of a new world, out of mankind, almost in spite of mankind. Our job, his as well as mine, is to liquidate things outworn. Catherine, let us confess the truth, we two men are obstetricians – no less and no more. We may kill the birth – yes, or we may save the birth, or cripple it, but I doubt if we can alter it in any other way. What has to be, has to be – in essence – whatever the accidents. What *he* has to say to his people is 'freedom and plenty – yes, but first,' he has to say, 'you must learn self-knowledge, public service, discipline.' What I have to say to my people is, 'authority and abundance – yes, but first you must give these common serfs, this cheated crowd, comfort, health, leisure, self-respect and individual hope. There is no authority but competence.' But the real forces that are shaping human life today and driving us all before them, are neither in politics nor business. They are in laboratories and drawing-offices on the one hand, and on the other in the spin of the earth, the dust before the wind, the blaze of the sun, the festering germs in the dirt. And certain incalculables. The true dictator of the world is an embracing necessity. Maybe the ultimate ruler will always be Necessity. Necessity presents us with opportunity. Take it or leave it, she says, but don't pretend to dictate. Whichever side wins or whether we two call it a draw and share the world, necessity will insist now, at the price of utter defeat for our race, upon much the same new industrial organization, much the same new monetary conventions, much the same new classifications of people, much the same distribution of work and leisure, much the same ways of travelling, much the same countryside and much the same education. Take it, she says, this new world, or refuse it and perish. Politicians like us are just the whippers-in of necessity. The old order breaks up, behaves preposterously. Dangerously. We too have behaved preposterously and dangerously until now here we meet face to face and see the truth through each other."

"Yes," said Catherine and stopped short.

They turned to her.

"There is still the old riddle," she said. "Who will control the rulers? Who will guard the guardians?"

"No one," said Bolaris.

Their silence seemed to question him.

"All balances and constitutions are provisional things. In the end when they are adult all men are irresponsible. We are going to do what we believe to be right."

"And if presently you give way to fatigue, fear, haste, hatred and anger, vanity?"

"So much the worse for the world and so much the worse for us. Maybe there will be others to take things out of our hands. But there is no helping that irresponsibility. We must judge ourselves now – we are adult men with nothing left to control us. Sovereign adult men. Or are you, Ratzel, still disposed to take orders from the Party?"

"About as much as you are disposed to die for your King?"

Catherine brooded. "Yes," she concluded. "That is what growing up means. You are men. And now, since this talk must come to an end, shall I make a foolish generalization about women? No woman has ever really respected a man who put a law or a leader or what you call love, above that innate sense – which is the very essence of manhood – of the right thing that he of himself has to do... Which is his necessity."

"Under God, the pious would say," said Ratzel.

"It is God," said Catherine.


Such in effect is what these two brothers and Catherine said and understood in their long talk, and that is the determination they drew out of each other. But the story-teller has stripped and simplified what they had to say and crossed the *t*'s and dotted the *i*'s, and smoothed out digressions and filled in several gaps that they with their innate intuitions were able to leap over.

A wordless treaty materialized between them as they talked. They had no doubt of themselves and each other.

4

Suddenly the air quivered with a renewal of the distant gun-fire and the thin bright orange thread of a signal rocket soared across the blue darkness. Both men stood up and looked towards the open window, listening.

Silence returned. There was not even the distant sound of an aeroplane. No conflagration was visible any longer nor the flash of any explosions. Maybe far away buried in that stillness, the wounded were being gathered in and the shattered posts and positions reconstituted. Nothing reached the three listeners.

"The cars are waiting," said Catherine. "What are we going to do?"

"You have to get back to your people, Ratzel. And I have to seize power tomorrow. Nothing can alter that."

"But how is he to get back to his people?" said Catherine.

"I haven't even a map," said Ratzel. "I don't know any of the ropes here."

Bolaris stood up. He walked to the window, whistling softly to himself and stood in a profound meditation. His shoulders showed Catherine that he was counting on his fingers, a trick he had when he was trying out some scheme.

He came back to the two seated at the table.

"This isn't going to be so easy," he said.

"The cars are waiting," she remarked.

"For the present, brother Robert, you must stay hidden here. Stand up and look resentful and a prisoner. Catherine, sit over there, and look at him as though he was poison." Bolaris clapped his hands for the guards and sent for the officer in command. A young man appeared and saluted. Bolaris scrutinized his face and decided to trust him.

"Something very responsible indeed," he said in a quietly impressive voice.

The young officer stiffened and tried not to look elated.

"This prisoner is very important. I want you to notice something. Just look at us as we stand together." He walked across to Robert, stood beside him for a moment and walked back. "That will do. Let him be taken away."

When Ratzel had departed with his guards Bolaris smiled mysteriously at his subordinate. "You noticed it?" he asked.

"The resemblance, sir. Yes."

"I have been trying to find out all I can about that individual. Something – never mind what – might arise out of this resemblance. I want you to guard him carefully, wait on him hand and foot so to speak, and learn his little ways. Let no one see him – absolutely no one – except yourself and the most trustworthy *stupid* men you have. Make him quite comfortable. I have an idea."

Bolaris acted hesitation, turned to Catherine. "Could I ask you to tell the cars to be ready downstairs," he said.

"I think I had better tell you my idea," he began, as soon as he and the young officer were alone. "It is a fantastic idea… I don't know you. But there is something about you inspires confidence. Suppose presently that man escapes and returns to the city and you help him to escape and go with him. No. Don't be shocked. Wait a moment. Suppose it was not really that man who escaped?"

Romantic excitement blazed in the young man's eyes.

"You mean, sir – ?"

"Yes. It might be necessary. Find out exactly who and what he is, so that if presently I choose to impersonate him... And you come with me... Do you understand?"

"Sir! Such an adventure!" He became speechless.

"Exactly. But now you see how it is no one must see him, no one. No one must come near him. It is my affair. This is the house of Madame Farness and you are her special guardian. It is a position of great responsibility. She knows – something. Not of course what I have told you about my intentions. If she wants to see that man she may do so. I doubt if she will. But let no one else come near him. Let no one know. No one – however important. Deny even that he is here. Can I trust you? Courage, loyalty, yes – but discretion?"

"Sir! – Try me."

"If any rumours get about – If there are too many fingers in this pie – "

"I quite understand, sir."

Bolaris held out his hand to the overwhelmed youngster.

"It is in your hands," he said.

"Keep your eyes open and say nothing," was his parting injunction to Catherine below. "Tell me anything out of the way that occurs. I shall be back as soon as I can. If you see him at all, see him discreetly. *Darling!*"

# CHAPTER FOUR

## Coups d'État

Events moved quickly at headquarters and the King's palace next day, and for the most part they went according to plan. Bolaris had the man of action's habit of keeping his thoughts in compartments, and his new philosophy of revolution and his project for restoring his brother to liberty remained disregarded in their pigeonholes until Gammet had been shot and the King, concealing his astonishment and dismay beneath a certain chilly graciousness, had acquiesced in Bolaris' assumption of supreme power. All the Five had played their appointed parts admirably. The *coup d'état* had been planned so well and was executed so neatly that it produced no visible breach in the Anti-Red front. On the afternoon of the second day the group, all its tasks accomplished, assembled in the former dining-room of the Orpedimento château, which was becoming now the council chamber of the new regime.

Bolaris kept them waiting for a time. It was his habit to keep them waiting and then appear with an air of having been working intensely on matters a little above and beyond them. But this time he stayed in his own large room upstairs, because he felt a

45

novel disinclination to go down to them. The agenda was plain and clear before him. The obvious next step was a concentrated culminating attack upon the Reds in the city, that would justify and consolidate his control. He wanted now to delay that ultimate attack as long as possible. He wanted to keep up an appearance of successful driving energy during a phase of essential ineffectiveness, while he worked out the new situation, the new situation within his mind quite as much as the military and political situation which had arisen in the past two days. He had to find plausible reasons for delaying his concentration and he had to make up his mind definitely about Ratzel, not only about his immediate escape but about their subsequent relations. For the two days of the *coup d'état* Ratzel had been, so to speak, in a pigeon-hole, now he had to come out again. And directly he was brought out again, he assumed the largest and most unmanageable proportions.

They were waiting downstairs.

He sat at the vast writing-desk of the Wine King, with its heavy silver equipment – even the three telephones were silver-mounted – and stuck out the fingers of his hand and tried to assign each one of them its particular part in the complex of his problem. But the fingers behaved as though they did not belong to one hand and refused to remain turned down.

"I do not want to take the city.

"But all my prestige depends upon taking the city.

"If Ratzel is killed, I can be in the city in a fortnight, and they know that as well as I do.

"*Do* they know that as well as I do? If I tell them that we underrate the spirit of the city and the support from outside that is still coming in?

"No. But if we take the city now – with all this foreign support behind us! Shall I tell them we must not take the city until we have our kind friends from abroad a little more in hand?"

That finger looked better than the others. It remained bent down.

"Next. Let us continue the patriotic strain. Assume that three-quarters of the city is patriotic *au fond*. Even if it doesn't know it…

"If I propose to double-cross our amiable allies by a deal with the Reds; How will they take it? Which do they hate most? We are supposed to be the patriotic side. But *are* we?

"Suppose – suppose I tell them I've got Ratzel and that he is a much more reasonable man than they suppose?

"Am I going to tell them I've got Ratzel?

"If I don't tell them now, it will be harder and harder to tell them.

"They will want him shot as publicly as possible, and from their point of view they will be right.

"How far can I afford to strain their confidence in me?

"I might have got Catherine to arrange his escape that very night. *Could* I have done that?

"No use crying over spilt opportunities. Somehow I must fix up some means of communicating with him and get him back to his proper place.

"I will tell them.

"I won't tell them."

He turned to his telephone and rang up Catherine. "I'm longing to see you," he said. "I'm damnably tired. I want every sort of consolation."

And then in Lampobo, "Use your mother-wit, my dear. I don't care how soon Ratzel gets back to his own side of the lines. I've no time to say anything more. Bless you, my dear."

"I'll try and see what can be done. It's difficult," she answered. "Bless *you*, my dear."

Bolaris took a turn up and down the room to recover his poise and then descended to the dining-room.

2

As Bolaris descended the florid and redundant staircase of the Wine King, a duplicated white marble affair lit patchily by big windows of modern stained glass, he was acutely conscious of an unusual indecisiveness and of an unusual sensibility. "I have been thinking," he said, very much as a man with a headache might say, "I have been drinking."

He had a queer feeling that he was not altogether there, as though something had been left behind with Ratzel, and exchanged for something else. Or as if long-neglected parts of his brain had been awakened to an unaccustomed activity. Or as if he had a new sort of stereoscopic vision, seeing round things a little because now he had two heads to see with. All sorts of things that had hitherto been irrelevant to him had assumed an air of not quite explicit significance, and things that he had hitherto gripped unhesitatingly as the business in hand had lost something of their lucid definition. It had never occurred to him before that the Wine King's palace was damnably vulgar, nor that it mattered in the least if it was. Now it came into his head that this pretentious superfluity of marble, with its mounted suits of European, West African and Japanese mail and its sham

Byzantine window saints, really did present something at which Ratzel could point a finger and say: "That's your capitalist system!"

It wasn't, of course...

Bolaris pulled himself back on the verge of a complicated internal argument, and passed between two saluting sentries into the big dining-room.

For an instant in the doorway, the staircase idea made a phantasmal reappearance. What a jumble of weak appeals to ancient prestige, unintelligent acquiescence in grandiose traditions and large unsubstantial claims to present importance, this room presented! The château of a wine-peddling, market-rigging merchant pretending to be a kingly palace! If any palace had ever been kingly! Could one ever hope to turn this sort of thing into a rational home for human beings? Maybe after all there was something to be said for revolutionary destructiveness, and beginning from the ground upward. While the upstairs room was silver this was all gilt. Over the fireplace was a vast pseudo-Correggio, very appetising for the diners, representing Elijah fed by the Ravens. The ceiling and walls were fussy with gilt pilasters, cornices, massive mouldings, suggesting imaginary thrusts against quite impossible strains. There was a number of big shining jars of porcelain, on brackets and pedestals. "The world has always been making big empty jars since Cnossos," he thought. "And sweating and enslaving and murdering to get them... A civilization of empty pots... The world made safe for crockery." These were preposterous ideas to have streaming across a mind that ought to have been clenched like a fist ready to deliver a blow. Criticizing furniture! A chandelier of crystal and gilt glittered from a ceiling rosette, and on either side of the huge hearth, gigantic ebony negresses sustained clusters of electric lights…

The Five, seated with a certain assumption of ease about the central table, were dwarfed by their surroundings. It looked as though they ought to have been larger or that there ought to have been more of them. He advanced across a shining floor space and they rose at his approach.

"Hail Chief!" said Handon. "You are master at last."

"Servus servorum," said Bolaris, standing at the head of the table. "The flag and social justice and our national honour."

"We look to you in all things," said Handon.

"And we have still to take the city," said Bolaris.

"But now we shall take it," said Handon. "Everything comes into your hands. Everything."

He seemed to be on the point of saying more. "Not yet," said Bolaris drily, and sat down and surveyed his associates. "Much has to be done before we recapture the city," he said, "and when we have taken it our troubles are only beginning…"

(What a lot they were! And what the devil was he going to tell them? Hitherto he had had the hard concentration of a sportsman when he handled them. He had liked it as one likes playing a game one can play well. He had lapsed long ago into the belief that this game was the best one could do with life; now he was alert with new doubts. Latterly he had fretted at his enslavement to his associates' loyalty, but that had not hampered his treatment of them; now he found himself simply and blindingly disliking and despising them. It would be difficult to control his irritation if anything adverse arose. Handon as usual had everything arranged for either action A, B, or C, but C meant extreme measures, and he did not want that for some time.)

He decided to make an apology in anticipation. "I've not slept for three nights," he said, and swept his hands over his face and stared again at his confederates.

What a lot! Who had said that? The voice of Ratzel echoed in his brain.

First there was Handon, his stalwart junior by three years, his devoted fag at school, his stooge during their student days, a relentless exacting admirer. Handon had a buoyant physique, an unlimited romantic imagination and a consciousness of intellectual inadequacy which did nothing whatever to limit his greed for power. Bolaris knew that Handon's hero-worship was largely self-projection. If the man could not dare to set up for dictator himself, the next best thing was to identify himself with the brilliant man who could. He wanted Bolaris to swagger with invincible resolution so that he could be a swaggering shadow. He was the sort of dog who bites the friends of those he loves. He could be counted upon for an unhesitating obedience to orders and an obstinate insistence upon what he considered his hero ought to do and be. Visibly he resented the existence of Catherine. He was bound to be extremely difficult about Ratzel.

Next to him sat the corpulent figure of Istom, the Big Money of the conspirators, the owner of the catalamite monopoly and the native partner in the foreign exploitation of the Gorram mines. His financial tentacles extended to London, New York, Amsterdam, and were hidden and camouflaged with extreme skill. His puffy face now radiated a genuine admiration for the success of Bolaris; he loved and made up to all successful fellows, but his eyes nevertheless had a certain watchful distrust. He was ready to give to the cause, he could give magnificently at times, but he was inflexibly hostile to taxation or control. He kept his own initiative. He was a born hider. So far Bolaris had never been able to find out what he hid nor how he hid things, nor what his understandings with his foreign partners were. How far would they come in to help him? Istom lived in great fear of the "Reds", and Reds for him were any people who seemed likely to impair that godlike sense of overpowering wealth which was his particular protection against the humiliations and frustrations of life. Without any visible physical preponderance those massive hoards of his gave him a sense of limitless power. You could intimidate men, play men through their greedy hopes, buy women – practically any woman – buy art, music, space. Provided your spending was uncontrolled. These Reds of his had no relation to the realities of "labour". They were conscience-born phantoms whose captain was Nemesis, and the core of the Anti-Red organization was an alliance of bold, cunning, able men, smaller or greater than himself, mostly, thank God, smaller. They were allied to defend their right, the right of the stronger to a free hand with their fellow creatures and an unchallenged survival for the winner. They did each other in a lot, good poker players all, but they kept a common front against the commonweal. "I serve his purpose while the Reds still fight," thought Bolaris. "But the day we are through with the shooting and killing and intimidation in the working-class quarters of the city, ends any use he has for me. It's him I want in handcuffs now. He knows that I mean to get his money at last if I have to cut through his knuckles. Unless he gets me first. He's no fool inside his fat white brain. He too is going to be difficult about Ratzel."

Close up to Istom, as if to assure himself and everyone else of their essential alliance, was the Duke of Carnavera Credora. He had that narrow aquiline face with large wandering features which is so frequent a result of aristocratic interbreeding. His chin was not an ordinary chin; it was an heirloom. His dark eyes were irregular and scornful, and the exquisite politeness of his manner to all the world was the quintessence of insolence. He had peculiarly long hands of which he was proud; he had a son who was a criminal cripple of which he was proud; he had a slight slobbery family lisp of which he was proud; he had syphilis so long inherited and so complicated that it had become less of a disease than a constitutional distinction of which he was proud. His estates covered vast areas, he had ancient castles and palaces and much rare furniture, historical jewels and priceless paintings, so that Istom's raw grandeurs and art patronage filled him with ill-concealed contempt. Not that he knew much about art, except that he knew that he was right about art and Istom wrong. Whatever he did was right and whatever Istom did was by natural necessity not. His ancestors glittered in history right back to the Byzantine Empire, and where were the Istoms then? He knew of no reason why the future should be different. He was convinced that the real people worshipped his family and were only being temporarily misled by agitators and suchlike mischief-makers, taking advantage of the irritation caused by Istom's excruciating lack of style.

No communist was as free from bourgeois prejudices as himself when it came to borrowing, defaulting, betraying, using and not paying. He would not scruple to sell his palaces, rare furniture, pictures, daughters, mistresses, to the highest bidder, confident that all things come back at last to the place where they belong. He believed Istom was saturated with snobbish admiration for aristocratic quality – or why should he covet palaces and titles? – and that he could twist him round his finger by drawling a little flattery, putting a hand on his shoulder and calling him "My dear Istom."

Just now – the Duke had to play a waiting game much as the King did. Why was he not with the King? Well – the King was a weak fool and suspicious in the wrong place. And besides, this so-called royal family was no better than the Duke's. Not nearly so good. Not an authentic trace of it before the eleventh century. And Bolaris? "Double-cross", was the Duke's maxim, "but never distrust." This fellow Bolaris was the sort of clever man you call in to do a job, just as you call in a physician, or an architect or a locksmith, or a lawyer, or one of those shuffling, respectful scientific oddities. Bolaris had to have a free hand for his cleverness. He had to be dictator. For a time. But dictators come and dictators go; they have no home life, no social tradition, no culture, no innate manners; while aristocracies go on for ever, the chronic beautiful disease, the hereditary syphilis of our species.

So Bolaris read him as he sat wearing his mask of aristocratic aloofness, his cynical detachment that hid nothing better in the way of reality than cunning, treachery and invincible conceit. Could he be detached from Istom? Not in the matter of Ratzel. Wherever the Left held the country, they had divided up the Duke's estates and filled his abject peasants with fantastic ideas about their rights. "My dear Bolaris!" the Duke had said, "the mischief of the social revolution is that they can do nothing properly. If they were better men than we, no one would be readier to hand things over than I. But how have they been be-having under the Revolution? They just sell my crops, keep no seed corn, gobble up the best pigs and eggs and seduce their own daughters. It was all so much better when it was done for them. Such a lot of the poor fellows will have to be killed, I'm afraid. Such a lot of them."

Not much help for Ratzel there.

Opposite the Duke was Fayle with his white face and his sunken dark eyes. The soul of Fayle had been a matter of profound speculation to Bolaris. He was a religious fanatic. He was an essential saint. He had sublimated his personality in the Church just as Handon had sublimated himself in the Leader. He had made the fretted exaltation of nave and aisle, the clustering still candles of choir and altar, the swinging censers, the chanting processions, the superhuman voice of the organ, the orderly functioning of service, fast and festival, the prescribed responses, the prescribed genuflexions and motions, his own, a necessary part of his bodily being. The mystery of pain in the crucifix, the pallid saints in chapel and window, stirred no mental processes in him but flushed him with profound spiritual emotion; he did not question them, did not think about them, but he gave himself unreservedly to them. He belonged to them and they to him, and the rest of the world had to prostrate itself to his mystical church self. Bolaris doubted whether he had the remotest idea of any God above himself or indeed of anything over and outside his Church. The Church was the wonderful, great and immortal Self he had achieved at the price of his meagre personality. He was only not a priest because he felt he could serve the Church better and get more out of it in political life. But he was a celibate, and his only use for women was that they should become saints and martyrs. Sex for him was a method of dominance over and persecution of natural desires, a cause for penitence and abasement.

To buy him Bolaris had "put the crucifix back in the schools", and it had been a poor bargain. Bolaris had hoped to use his fanaticism against the King's frivolity, against the exploitation of the workers and the oppression of the peasants, but he had underrated the exalted detachment of Fayle's spirituality. The spectacle of deprived and downtrodden human beings aroused envy in him rather than pity, for while he wore his hair short with an effort, God saw to theirs. And Ratzel had let his atheist following defile relics, mock at priests, insult nuns and burn magnificent churches. If Fayle could not hope for a complete restoration of his sacred buildings, there was at any rate the belated wrath of God upon Ratzel to anticipate. No help there.

Lastly, on Bolaris' right sat that stout old soldier, Goodamanas, his father's companion in arms, a gallant lout. He lived not for "service" indeed or anything so abstract, but for the Services. He wanted the army to be a shining sword and his imagination went no further. Anything that might diminish it, impair its clean brightness, hamper its swiftness, question it in any way, was anathema to him. This, too, was self-projection, but free of the queer sexualized complexities of Fayle. He was chivalrous, he was patriotic; on one or two occasions he had even admired the strategy of "that red devil" in the city. He was for the dictatorship – and keeping the King in his place – simply out of his hopeless contempt for the royal personality and because of the King's bad treatment of his niece. The King had shown no *esprit de corps*, he was an entirely unworthy hilt for the national blade.

Goodamanas had no professional vanity. He had never betrayed hate or affection for Bolaris, but he had played a straight game with him and accepted his leadership without cavil because it was more competent than his own. After all the son of General Bolaris, legitimate or not, was one of his caste. His grip could be firm but it was never malignant. His attitude to Ratzel might not be a foregone conclusion, and there is nothing military men dislike so much as the practice of shooting antagonistic generals. Bolaris counted; himself, one, Handon, trustworthy but troublesome, two, and a doubtful Goodamanas, three; something might be done if as Dictator he grabbed the casting vote.

Such was the core of the dust eddy of thought that whirled through the mind of Bolaris, in the brief pause before he began to speak.

3

"I want to put my views and intentions about this new situation in which we find ourselves, as clearly as possible. It is vital that we should have the completest understanding among ourselves about how things stand, about what we are doing and what we are going to do. Our armies have had a defeat but, to be frank, it is a defeat that is not without its redeeming aspects. It has rid us of a lamentable division of command, and it is not upon our own nationals that the brunt of the loss has fallen. We still hold the initiative in this war and there has been no loss of morale; indeed the reverse has drawn us all together more closely than ever in our common devotion to the Cause of God, King and Country."

He bowed his head, and his five associates, with an equal sincerity, bowed in sympathy.

"You are saying this in your proclamation?" said Istom.

Bolaris smiled. "Precisely. And it sounds like a proclamation. I prepared that this morning. And now let us get down to some underlying realities that are bound to come to the surface directly the city is in our effective occupation. For I assure you I can certainly be in the city in a fortnight – almost certainly in ten days – and then what?"

"A general clean-up," said Istom. "Reconstruction of industry – business. Solvency will not wait. We have been fighting our way deep and deeper into debt. Production has slowed down. It has been like a heart stopping."

"One or two things take precedence of that."

"The churches, the schools," said Fayle.

"Even of that," said Bolaris.

"The land, I suppose, can wait – and the crops and the seasons," sneered the Duke with manifest irony.

"First of all," said Bolaris, "we want to be masters in our own house. Our friends from the North East have been landing more troops, more material – as you know. If I get into the city in ten days, I shall be there with a tired army with its hands full – and our kind friends, as fresh as paint, will be ready to take anything over that they can. We have to remember they have allies in high quarters."

"Pin-head is a fool and a traitor," said the Duke. "We all know that."

"We may have them on our backs for the next twenty years," said Bolaris.

"We couldn't perhaps give them the place of honour in our next attack?" suggested Goodamanas.

"We cannot do that twice," said Bolaris.

"And so we have to wait again!" cried Handon, and was again on the verge of saying more.

"No," said Bolaris. "We have to be in the city – in a fortnight."

"But *how* – ?" began Istom.

Bolaris held up his hand and paused for a moment before he made his announcement.

"I have had, in an irregular and unexpected way, a communication from Ratzel."

An idea flashed into Bolaris' head as he spoke. Instead of admitting that he had Ratzel, he might represent his prisoner as a messenger from Ratzel. But Handon might make that difficult. No time to think that out now. He became aware of the intent eyes upon him.

"Ratzel," he invented, "wants to make a deal."

"We must take the city," said Goodamanas.

"The city could be abandoned for us to march in," said Bolaris, still romancing. "On terms."

"What terms?" said Fayle.

"Yes. What terms?" said the Duke.

And Istom turned the silent beam of a full-faced interrogation upon Bolaris.

"Man is by nature a patriot," began Bolaris.

"How can Ratzel be patriotic?" said Fayle. "He is an American."

Bolaris disregarded that. "The mass of the people in the city are primarily patriotic," he said. "It is the only form in which they are really capable of thinking of themselves as a community. That's as far as they have grown up. The great point made against us is our foreign alliance."

"What terms would Ratzel offer?" said Fayle.

"He will drop the Red flag."

"Good," said Goodamanas, to whom flags meant much, but the others were not so easily satisfied. Their faces remained expectant.

"All things come to an end and give place to fresh," said Bolaris. "The Red flag has meant tremendous things in people's imaginations. But now it is played out."

"What has it ever meant but envy of success on the part of the incapables?" said Istom.

"Hatred of God," said Fayle.

"The snarl of the natural slave who does not know his place," said the Duke. "I thought Aristotle had settled all that."

"Aristotle said there were natural slaves," Bolaris reflected. "But I doubt if he ever really consulted any natural slaves about it."

"Why *should* he?" said the Duke in a half aside. "And if there was anything else in the Red flag at any time, what was it?"

"*Hope*," said Bolaris. He realized that he was being drawn into an argument, that he was not tellings things to these people in good dictatorial style but pursuing novel lines of thought springing out of his colleagues' self-revelations. He was not trying to dominate them. He was not trying to convince them. He was trying to state novel ideas that had invaded and changed his mind. It was as though an entirely new system was struggling for the possession of him. His clear-cut decisiveness had deserted him.

"For the last century or more, this idea that life could be made abundant without a stroke of work, free meals and free circuses and everybody better off than anyone else, human subjugation abolished, has been spreading through the world like a contagious disease," said the Duke. "God knows where it will take us. It is so terribly plausible to the inexperienced; it is so fundamentally absurd. What *is* civilization but balance, refinement, selection?"

"The damnedest of all heresies," said Fayle, "is the belief in progress, the denial of the necessary limitations of the normal human life."

"That hope," said Bolaris, "– the Red flag I mean – was the sense of a promise, the first brightness of a dawn."

"My dear fellow," said the Duke, "this is like one of the spouters of the other side. What sort of dawn are you thinking of? What sort of new sun is this which will rise in the west, and reverse all the precedents of nature?"

"Spouters?" said Bolaris, and abruptly something seemed to turn over in his mind. These people were unbearable. All capacity, all disposition to persuade and humour these uncongenial associates deserted him in a blaze of indignation. Yet still he tried to control himself and the Five. "And you really think," he asked, "that that hope, that belief in progress, which as you say has been running like an infection about the world for the space of three lifetimes, can ever be quenched again?"

"Certainly," said the Duke, "isn't that what we are trying to do now, and can anything else in the world be done but that? '*Hope*' of this sort has always been cropping up and needing suppression. Inequality is the first law of human nature."

"The law of God," said Fayle.

"The kindest thing," said the Duke, "the very very kindest thing you can do to your natural inferiors is to keep them in their places. I know it. I'm not without experience. This will-o'-the-wisp of irrational desires and impossible vindications which you call hope, may be in full flow; all the more need for strength and firmness. The swifter and grimmer the lesson, the less the suffering. If we do not beat out this spirit of mass rebellion, trample on it now, destroy the faintest hope of any recovery, it will begin all over again. Who was it said, 'the price of civilization is eternal vigilance'?"

Fayle decided not to correct the misquotation.

"I agree," said Istom.

"We cannot afford to consider terms with the Reds," said the Duke. "We must dictate them, or our social order will collapse in hopeless ruins. It has been the growth of ages and ages of evolution, it is a whole system, a system of tried and tested balances we inherit, and there is nothing, nothing whatever, to replace it. Nothing. There is no other social order *possible*. That is what none of you world-menders realize. As well try and abolish the headship of the head, and surrender things to a dictatorship of the guts. Don't blame me, my dear Bolaris. It isn't I who made the world like this; it is the way the world is made, kings and priests, rich and poor, gentle and simple – so it has been from the beginning, so it must always be."

"But," said Bolaris. And then with a wrathful wrench of his mind flung out of this argumentative groove altogether. "Never have I heard such nonsense. Never yet have I had to tolerate such useless talk from grown men. You seem to think that nothing changes in human possibility. Because otherwise where would you be? I tell you that everything has changed. I tell you that within a century age-old mists of ignorance and misconception have been scattered like clouds before the sunrise. It *is* a dawn, it is illumination. What is the good of sneering at these words, Duke, because they have been worn threadbare? That does not make them untrue. The eyes of the common man have been opened. He has such a conception of what life may be as no nobleman had five hundred years ago. Maybe he is still like that man who was given sight and saw men like trees walking. That will pass. Whatever else arrives we are going on into a clear-sighted world. The common man will not stand life as you lucky ones dole it out to him any longer. You had no generosity in your minds. You failed to make your peace with him when you were in the way with him. You will be able to humbug him less and less; and you will exasperate him more and more. Make your suppressions harsher and harsher; they break in your hands. The crowd may not be able to replace the old conditions by new ones quite possibly, but rest assured if its conditions are not replaced, it will smash them, even if smashing them means disaster, collapse – utter destruction for our species. Get that idea right; it is the fundamental reality in things today. Let me say it again, Duke, in spite of that suppressed yawn. The endurance and discipline of common people is at an end; they will never stand the old conditions again; they may embrace violent and ineffective doctrines, they may believe blindly for a time in the promises of this new leader or that, they may cease to struggle on for a time and try to get back to some imaginary golden age, kings again for a bit, dictators, prophets. They may commit infinite follies, but unless they get change and satisfying change, they will break and perish rather than submit, and you and I will go into the boiling with them. This pretty historical world of yours, of kings and priests, lords and ladies, rich and poor, is going to pieces under your very eyes. It can never be put back again, never. The harder you try to hold it together the more it will rot and change. You might as well dream of restoring the stink of horse droppings to the avenues of New York or repeopling roads with the chariots of Ur. You people are as incapable of maintaining the old order of things as those rebels and doctrinaires away there in the city are of setting up a new. Of that anyhow you are all quite sure; aren't you? We are as much in the revolution as those you call the Reds – far more. What I stand for, and what until today I always believed you understood I stood for, is a new order of things without a precedent, and if we also on our side cannot evoke the necessary vigour and the imagination and above all the generosity for a new order of things, then social collapse will continue indefinitely. That is not simply our case in this country. It is the plain destiny before all the world.

"No. No. Don't fret, Istom, listen to me. I used to think you and your business rationalization and so on had at least a bit of creativeness about it. Are you, too, for just sticking it, in the mud and blood here?

"This new order, Istom, we have to make must be newer and stronger than any of the dream worlds they imagine over there. *Their* whole turn of mind is to insubordination and sabotage. What else could it be? Their Utopias are infantile. They have never known anything but limitation. We have to go one better than they can. The only possible reply to a poor rebel revolution is going right on to a better and bigger creative revolution, and that means a new order of things altogether."

"Well, that's your corporate state!" said Istom.

"Mm-m!" said the Duke. "Hobbes' dear old Leviathan come ashore – with Istom in control."

"The only possible corporate state is to have the whole of mundane affairs under the direct control of the Church," said

Fayle. "Restore Christendom! The guidance of God and the wisdom of the ages."

Bolaris went on talking as though these things had not been said. What they were doing in each case, except maybe Handon's, was, he knew, to think these terrifying words "a new order of things altogether" into the form of their heart's desires, a little brighter and larger. "Your corporate state, Istom," he said, "was a tawdry first attempt to exploit the new necessities, a mere vague gesture towards that complete scientific socialism which is the only possible escape from social disintegration."

"Not socialism exactly," said Istom. "That's where I differ."

"Not scientific," said Fayle. "Christian."

"You played with it a little, Istom, and then you dropped it," said Bolaris. "It went on beyond your courage and will. All the same that possible new order is taking shape in men's imaginations; its necessary conditions are growing clearer. Men have to go on with their minds; they have to go on – and on. Go on to the new. Only by the complete abandonment of current ideas and current antagonisms can the new world be brought into being. Not only vast changes in institutions but changes in general ideas, changes in moral conceptions, a new universal education." (Fayle shook his head.) "Yes – a new religion, an incessantly progressive religion, a reconstruction of behaviour, clearer and clearer ideas of property and social reward. All that. If you are not prepared for that much creation then you are no better than those mere rebels over there; you too are men who refuse to learn; tearing at this dying social system – which must die anyhow, from a different point and at a different angle...

"Oh! Get on with it. Get on with the new world. Stop your poor defensive resistances. Enlightenment, clarification – trite

65

words, my dear Duke, eh? but alive where you are dead! Remould this world nearer the shape of men's new dreams and desires. Yes, that means something. It means everything above the level of an everlasting fight for front place at the hog-trough. Ratzel, I know – never mind how I know – has come to realize that, as clearly as I do; he is willing to help and he has got to help. This imbecile civil warfare of sham loyalties, stale dogmas, perverted traditions and fragmentary ideas has got to end. He's a man with a brain like mine, and the sooner we can get in touch with him the better for us all."

"No!" said the Duke.

"No! Atheists and murderers!" said Fayle.

"How far will he come away from Communism?" asked Istom.

"Now you know where I stand," said Bolaris, "and the way I mean to go. There it is. Either you come on with me... Men, where do you think we are going? Where else is there to go?"

4

He met doubt and antagonism in their eyes, even in the eyes of Handon and Goodamanas. His train of thought ceased to flow, crystallized, lit up and became resolution.

The unwonted thinker in him gave place to the natural fighter. His expression became cheerful. "That's how we stand, that is what we have to do."

He smiled and stared them in the face.

"Now," said Istom, "after this magnificent flight into the ideal, let us come down to practical realities. I have always been open to the idea of – rationalization. Of a kind. Reasonable rationalization.

Profit sharing. Controlled marketing. Rationing. We are all socialists nowadays and all that. What in concrete fact does Ratzel offer us and what at the present time are we going to do?"

He went unanswered.

"We are going to make a firm deal with Ratzel," said Bolaris. "The city is going to surrender. We are going to help our foreign allies to pack up and facilitate their departure."

Fayle made a dissentient noise.

"Now is the time for ending this imbecile war of the Lefts and Rights, this bloodshed for nothing. Everywhere men are war-weary. All the world is tired of a state of siege. Now is the time for the new unity – with Ratzel in the mood for it."

"With Ratzel in our hands!" said Handon abruptly. He could contain himself no longer.

5

"With Ratzel in our hands!"

Bolaris could have struck his right-hand man.

For some vivid moments it was as if Bolaris was the defendant in a trial instead of a dictator. Three faces accused him. Handon was dismayed already at his own precipitance. Goodamanas sat rigid, profoundly perplexed, trying to be firm and rigid *in vacuo*.

"What are you going to do with him?" asked Istom.

"Where is he?" asked Fayle.

"Where have you put him?" demanded the Duke.

"I have him where I want him," said Bolaris. "When we have fixed our deal with him I am going to send him back."

"Send him back!" cried Istom.

"Shoot him!" said the Duke.

Fayle murmured approval. "The Church does not execute. But it acquiesces."

"It is absolutely necessary that we should come to an agreement with Ratzel if ever social order is to be restored. This fools' war now I tell you is like the Thirty Years' War – a fantastic waste of the human generations."

"I mistrust Ratzel," said Handon.

"Think what will happen if he does not return to them," said Bolaris, like a grown man talking to unreasonable pupils. "We shall have no one to deal with."

"So much the better," said the Duke. "They will break up."

"Yes, yes, but think what that really means! These people are indignant. They have reason to be indignant. Every common man in the world now is justly and properly indignant with human life – their vague indignations have been drawn together. No one can completely satisfy them, but Ratzel has given their angry discontent with life a form with which we can deal. He is the one man they trust not to betray them."

He overrode their protests. "What is the good of argument? If you do not follow me in this – you will never take the city. This war has to end and I and Ratzel alone can end it."

"I do not trust Ratzel," Handon repeated.

"It is not my affair to criticize," said Goodamanas. "I have accepted the leadership of Bolaris and I and my Bands and indeed all the army now are with him. I doubt. So far as I understand I disagree. But I serve."

"I too," said Handon, not to be outdone in loyalty, "and my Boys and the Inner Circle. We stand by the Captain."

There was a momentary pause.

"*Well?*" said Bolaris, turning to the recalcitrants.

"This is militarism," said Istom, "naked and unashamed. This is the end of democracy."

"Like so many of your American friends," said Bolaris, "when you say democracy you mean unfettered finance, private police, controlled newspapers and so on. You have no idea of service. *Your* democracy is a jungle in which you prowl and scheme against mankind. From henceforth, Istom, either you will play your game with glass pockets and cards down on the table or you won't play at all."

Istom stood up sharply and immediately the Duke rose beside him, but Fayle understood the situation better and remained seated, passive and obdurate.

"Then it has to be C," said Bolaris to Handon.

Handon turned to the guards and muttered an order. Fresh men who had been waiting in readiness appeared.

"A council in time of crisis must be unanimous," said Bolaris.

"Absolutely," said Goodamanas.

"And that means?" asked the Duke.

"A temporary close on all discussion."

"We are dismissed?"

"No. You are retained. There must be no conflict outside this room. People's minds out there are in a state of tension. Your lives will not be safe."

"That's not the fact," said Fayle.

"Under a dictatorship – in times of urgency, fact is as the dictator wills. You will be held *incommunicado*. But in the utmost comfort."

"I also?" said Istom.

"You most of all," said Bolaris, and gave Handon the signal.

Istom looked more like an apoplectic frog than ever. "To think that I walked into this!"

## 7

"And now they have gone, my Captain," began Handon.

"You approve?"

"You have put Private Finance and Landlord and Church in their places and cleared your way. So far I am absolutely yours. I did not expect it like this, but I see now it had to be swift and absolutely unexpected. And now – ?"

"I am no politician," said Goodamanas.

"I do not want to hide anything from you," said Bolaris, playing for time, "but in this business I must have a free hand."

"About Ratzel," said Handon, "I should like to know."

For the moment Bolaris could not think quickly enough. "I want him to seem to escape," he said.

"A false escape?"

"But how can you trust him? What guarantee can you have he will not trick you?"

Bolaris lost his head for a moment and committed himself. "The best guarantee," he said. "*I* shall go to the city, and if by any chance they realize what has happened, he will be hostage for me."

Handon threw up his hands. "It is impossible. There are a thousand dangers and difficulties."

Bolaris laid a reassuring hand on his shoulder. "Which we meet as they arise, Handon. Trust me."

# CHAPTER FIVE

## The Tangle

Bolaris found himself regretting acutely the lost mental simplicity of two days ago. Then he had nothing but straightforward crookedness in his mind, a game to play as strictly limited in its rules as a game of chess. He had had the clearest conception of the side he was on and the antagonists he had to defeat in turn. But now the chess pieces were changing colour, the board was expanding and contracting, the chequer work grimacing in fantastic patterns. He was no longer for or against Right or Left. The infection of Ratzel's too congenial mind had made all these antagonisms transparent and unreal. Beneath them had appeared a conception of reality that made them incredible and crazy. He saw nothing now with a single eye; he had become stereoscopic.

It was the Ratzel influence that had precipitated this open conflict with Istom, Fayle and the Duke. He had contemplated no such breach. His intention had been to sustain a policy of thrust and pressure and qualified reconciliation with them, and even to conclude at last with a compromise between their practical realities and the complete realization of his corporate theories. Even as his ends had grown more downright and definite, his purpose had still remained one of steadfast encroachment rather than antagonism. Now that intention was smashed. Handon's disclosure of Ratzel's capture had exploded that. There could be no more of that unfriendly alliance. He had struck openly at them, and now there was nothing for it but to go on striking. He had them under arrest; at the utmost he could keep that secret only for a few hours. There had been no one in immediate attendance upon them, but their cars would have to be sent back, and their staffs, households and adherents would be missing them and alert at the latest by tomorrow morning. Then he would have to go on to wholesale arrests.

The best thing he could think of was that the entire council, with the exception of Goodamanas, should vanish at the same time. All five, it could be whispered, had gone away very secretly upon an affair of state. Something to do with the King. That would create a mystification, but it would not suggest a breach.

Meanwhile he must get Ratzel back to the city. How?

He had got the young officer prepared for the fantastic idea of his impersonating Ratzel. He had got Handon in a state of protesting complicity with the same idea. On the spur of the moment that had seemed to him a dazzlingly brilliant idea, but since then his imagination had produced one possible complication after another. He could pass muster perhaps in the city, though a whole crop of hitherto unthought of difficulties arose as he worked out details, but now with his own council in violent conflict how could Ratzel hope to impersonate him? How could Ratzel handle the changing emergencies of the next forty-eight hours at the château? It would be far better if he got back in control on his own side... What were Catherine's quick wits doing down there at the villa? Had she hit upon any fresh way out? That young officer would sit on his prey now like a watch-dog.

Bolaris ticked off necessary items.

"He must have a complete set of my clothes.

"At the last moment he must shave and Catherine must clip his hair.

"I must have not only his clothes down there but another set of my own. Then I can be Bolaris or Ratzel as occasion arises.

"Somehow we must get this stuff into a room with ourselves. We must have that youngster waiting outside. On some excuse. What excuse? Catherine must help there. I must keep in the background away from the light as Ratzel. Ratzel must come out as me. He'll take that. He knows Ratzel's movements by this time and he hardly knows anything of me... I might contrive a recognizable scratch on my neck. I must arrange a feather of hair at the back of my head...

"Is there any other way? A plain straightforward escape? Catherine will know that by this time.

"Will a rope be useful? Hooks?

"Shall I take Handon? Yes. No.

"These are only preliminaries. What else can I do? Is there anything else I ought to take? I must get down there at once."

He decided to take Handon with him. Goodamanas was the only man in the world he would have dared to leave in control behind him. He called for Handon to get the cars, and then turned to his telephone to talk Lampobo with Catherine. She told him something very cheerful.

"This villa was part of the old convent. It is cavernous underground and two passages run away under the ruined wing of the hospital. I've worked out some things. Need I say more now?"

"Less. I'm starting to you right away," he said.

2

"Do you really mean to go through with this?" asked Handon in the car.

"Let me try it out in my imagination anyhow," said Bolaris. "In the end I may be largely guided by you. You must see us together, him and me, again."

"If you are guided by me – " began Handon, and left it at that.

Presently he asked: "What have you got in that big portmanteau?"

"My dear Handon, you are not a married man," laughed Bolaris.

"Sorry," said Handon.

"We must be back before nightfall," reflected Bolaris. "Nothing can happen up here until then. By the by, have you eaten?"

"I had some sandwiches."

"I wish I had brought some. I forget all about food. I haven't touched a mouthful today. Madame Farness will have to give me something…"

Again silence. Then Bolaris thought aloud. "We've had no planes over this side for three days. I wish I knew what that meant? It's a general lull… What a perfect siesta! Half those fellows down among the tents there might be asleep. Most of them are. That last gate was slow to open and the man looked scared. He hoped we didn't see he hadn't his boots on and that he had been as fast asleep as a dormouse."

"I'd have told him off," said Handon, "if we'd had the time."

Bolaris returned to his private thoughts.

If Catherine had really found some sort of bolt-hole and secret passage, then the problem was simply to get the young officer out of the way, form an accurate idea of how far Ratzel could get before he had to come out in the open, and what sort of situation he would come out into. "Damn!" said Bolaris suddenly. He ought to have had a Black Legion uniform available. But after all that might save Ratzel from the Anti-Red only to get shot at by his own side...

"What?" said Handon.

"How – what?"

"Why *damn?*"

"I'm so damnably hungry," said Bolaris.

"*I* ought to have thought of sandwiches," said Handon, full of self-reproach.

(But *would* they shoot him? They'd think he was a deserter...

What exactly had Catherine found? She was resourceful. She would have thought out plans...)

"All this corner is very badly charted," he said aloud to Handon. "Have we anyone who knows the lie of the ground beyond the ravine?... We have to have these gaps. It would need half a million men to hold this circle round the city, and I suppose neither we nor they total a hundred thousand. They can't afford men for anything serious this way. They hold us and we hold them. All the same – "

"Yes," said Handon.

"I wonder what Ratzel was looking for when we caught him!"

He took out and unfolded a sketch map. "See that spur from the ravine? Round here behind the convent. Vague, isn't it? I should feel safer if I knew that a little more precisely. Have you anyone – ?"

Handon looked at the map. "I could see to that myself," he said.

3

Bolaris sat in Catherine's room with an untouched meal on a tray before him. "Handon," he said, "prides himself on his intuitions in scouting; thank Heaven. So we are quit of him for an hour or so. And now – I want Ratzel to escape."

"You've given up that idea of impersonating him?"

"Absolutely. Catherine, it was childish. Ratzel must escape as Ratzel – all we can do is to give him a gun. I've been over-obsessed by that impersonation idea. But as we try it over we realize how weak it is. It's boyish. It's as impossible as the *Comedy of Errors*. It's *Prisoner of Zenda* romance. It just leapt up in my mind and it has entangled me ever since. Dismiss it. Tell me now – exactly. How can he escape?"

Catherine put her elbows on the table and spoke compactly and to the point.

Ratzel's room, she explained, was below the ground level. It opened into a sunken area covered by a grating over which a sentry had been placed. Catherine had watched him from her window above. He interpreted his instructions liberally, especially in the afternoon, when he would often be snoozing on a bank of violets under a stone angel, a score of yards away. In one corner of the area was a water tap and a big sink with an escape grating below, that Ratzel had found quite easy to loosen and lift. From it a quite climbable shaft descended to the main cloaca of the villa, and this again led to a tunnel that forked and ran south and east under the walls of the old convent part of the hospital. From the forks there were openings to an old moat outside, choked with agaves and litter, and thence overgrown rain gullies led down to the head of the ravine. There seemed to be no sentinels in that direction. It had not been thought of. Ratzel's prison had been improvised, and no very exact consideration had been given to the possibilities of an escape. The young officer was in and out whenever he thought proper, and there were two men in the room next to him but they too were inconstant guardians. The young officer would send one or both of them away on errands and they were relieved by others. They were unaware of the importance of the captive.

There would be no great difficulty in getting as far as the ravine if the attention of Ratzel's particular bodyguard could be detached for an hour or so. That youngster was the essential difficulty. Some way down the ravine, so far as she had been able to observe, there were two or three small outposts, part of a thin line which connected up to a few observation points and machine-gun nests on the edge of the woods that covered the mountain-side, which otherwise was unoccupied. Beyond was an indefinite arid no-man's-land of rock and cactus. The whole of the further country was waterless and uncultivated. No one seemed to know what ground the Reds were holding nor in what strength. They might be twenty miles away or more.

"Evidently what we have to arrange," said Bolaris, "is the get-away here. After that he can take his chances. What have you schemed for that?"

"He will want a pistol and a water-bottle," said Catherine. "That's not difficult. The only serious difficulty is the vigilance of your young officer here. You have excited him about this business beyond all measure...

"Richard, why do you excite people? Why do you inspire them? He's crazy to go with you to the city. He'd go with you straight into the Arabian Nights. Why have you that fatal attraction for people of limited imagination? You draw them like a magnet. There is such a candour about you, such a real friendliness and such a self confidence. Something arises in them and shouts 'Now I need not manage this life of mine any more. Now I need not bother about this perplexing world again. To this man I will give myself. His right shall be my right and his wrong my wrong. His success shall be mine – and he is sure of success.' And after that you never shake them off. They encumber you – as women do. As I do."

"Not you."

"I've not had a mind of my own since you began to trail me after you. Well, he is as devoted to you now as Handon, and between them you are like a prisoner between two guards. They mean you to be the champion of the Anti-Reds, the saviour of society from all that Red awfulness – whatever it is. I've seen you stepping right out of those ideas in the last few days, but how can *they* understand that? Never will they let you change, never will they let you go. Well, anyhow I don't *enslave* you."

"You don't enslave me," he said. "Dearest, you are the best of lovers – a lover without expectation."

"I have more than I ever expected," she said. "But let us be practical. Both your young officer and Handon have entered into this idea of an impersonation and a seizure of Ratzel's power over the Left organizations. The boy is frantic to do it. Handon hates the idea and will prevent it if he can. But he believes you mean it. The practical outcome is that the boy sticks to Ratzel like a leech, sits talking to him and watching him, seems jealous even of leaving me alone with him. Ratzel likes him and talks to him. I think he misunderstands his – adhesiveness. He thinks he has made a convert. He talks to him of much the same things as you would now, about civilization, about your universal liberal world order and so on, and the youngster finds what he says at once attractive, and since it is tinted Red, indescribably wicked... Never mind all that now, dear. I run on because I'm trying to keep pace with you. The point is that Ratzel cannot get away until you separate him from his keeper, and the only way to separate them is for you to go on to a certain extent with that impersonation idea. I've puzzled it out. He'll only leave Ratzel's side naturally and unsuspiciously when he starts with you for the city. So I see nothing for it but for you to make a show at least of changing clothes and starting."

"But how?"

"Listen."

"I listen."

"We call up your bright young officer boy and give him the change of clothing and so on you have brought with you. Then you go down with him to Ratzel, and with his assistance you and Ratzel change clothes. None of the men must know of this. He sends them away. You say you are a little doubtful after all whether it is a good impersonation. You decide to make the attempt. You and the young officer come up from the cellar and go into the big room beside the hall. There is no reason for leaving anyone at all down there. If there are any soldiers about down there they can have a glimpse of Ratzel in your clothes standing out of the light in the prison room, smoking a cigar and reading a map or something of that sort. They think that is you. You are not their affair, and it will be quite easy for our officer to get them out of the way. *Then* he locks up Ratzel and takes you to one of the small rooms upstairs. You discuss a pseudo-escape with him very gravely and in detail, and meanwhile Ratzel is really escaping downstairs. Then you begin to doubt whether you ought not to go alone to the city. He will be terribly disappointed. Ratzel is locked in and nobody in particular is looking after him because nobody knows about that drain. You tell your young officer you must see Handon. You send the young man off to find Handon and you remain under guard. The guards think you are Ratzel and are content, and the real Ratzel has already wriggled half-way down the sink shaft."

"Good," said Bolaris, "so far. Very good. But what next? Having Ratzelized me you have to get me unRatzelized again."

"When Handon returns he will certainly protest against this wild freak of yours."

"If he sends anyone downstairs? They will find Ratzel has gone."

"Why should he send anyone downstairs? That will be giving away your disguise to the men, and the less people who know of that the better. Meanwhile I am watching from upstairs and I get busy. I will ring up your secretary at the château, do a quick talk, and come flying downstairs or wherever you are with an urgent message from Goodamanas for you personally. Something has happened. Trouble at the palace. He wants you as soon as possible."

"And then?"

"Hustle. Extreme hustle. The cars are called and you carry off Handon and the young officer together."

"With Ratzel forgotten! No, dear. Trust Handon not to forget him. I agree to your general plan, but listen. Why not this? So soon as the guards and the young officer are upstairs, Ratzel, who is for the time being Bolaris, walks through the guardroom and – can he get out that way?"

"In your clothes he could, I suppose, walk right past a sentinel if necessary and slip down – there is a place there – into the old tunnel. But then – there's more risk. He might run against Handon or the young officer. No, no, my way is best. We spring a sort of wild hustle-scurry, and then if Handon does find Ratzel has escaped, what can he do? It will seem plain prison-breaking. Nobody is going to see just how unobtrusively we've made it possible. And while the guards here are hunting about for Ratzel you are off to the castle – more and more yourself again. You make no attempt to act. You give orders. Nobody will think much of your changed clothes. You often contrive to be pretty dirty, and when you are up there you can change into a uniform."

"The youngster will be mad. He'll want to stay back here and hunt Ratzel."

"He can."

"I think it works," said Bolaris. "And now we must tell Ratzel."

4

Ratzel with his habitual dry smile sat down between them, and as soon as the guards were out of the room Bolaris recapitulated the details for the escape.

Ratzel nodded. He asked a few questions. "All that seems to work very well. It's got to be done. Your little officer boy is almost oppressively conscientious and adhesive. Otherwise he's remarkably likeable. He admires you. Me, he regards as *sinister*. He feels that if he stops watching me for a moment I may inject some Red poison into him unbeknown. The more reasonable he finds the things I say, the more insidious he feels they are. Of course I am to change clothes with you under compulsion. Good! It's all clear. You'll slip me a revolver as we change. Sure we can do that?…"

"The water-bottle will be put in the room now," said Catherine. "I'll see to that myself."

"And tomorrow night," said Ratzel, "I shall be restoring order in the city and you will be – ?"

"Having some trouble up above here," said Bolaris. "But I've got the armed forces well in hand. There may be a bit of shooting…"

"And then in the name of patriotism we call a truce and get rid of your foreign friends. And after *that?*"

"We carry on our truce – in the name of civilization."

"A new civilization."

Bolaris was turning things over in his mind.

He laughed. He began talking.

"So at last," he said, "after a world of trouble you and I find out that we have both been serving the Common Fool – the normal human animal who quarrels by nature, can tolerate no superiority and hates new things. The left and right in any age are just the two faces of the Common Fool, and nothing more, and you have been on one face and I the other. Your Communist fool denounces what he calls Utopianism and my Individualists denounce Socialism. And when we look into it they mean precisely the same thing. What moves them either way is fear and hatred of the unknown, fear and hatred of the coming scientifically organized state, dread that they will be called upon for effort and performance. Your Communist releases his fear and detestation of anything whatever that isn't the glorification of his proletarian self, through the class-war and his blind hatred of what he calls Utopians, and my Individualist does exactly the same thing by denouncing the collective control that would stop his grabbing and gripping, and hating what he calls visionaries and fanatics. Both Left and Right are defensive hate systems. Both are obdurately dogmatic. Both pretend to be 'scientific' and both suppress reason. Neither will face novelty. The further we recede in time from them, the more we realize how identical they are. Marx stinks of Herbert Spencer and Herbert Spencer stinks of Marx. They are the great unimaginative twins. And here we are, Ratzel! The imaginative twins. What have you and I, whose minds are open and incessant, who are adventurers in spirit and innovators in grain, what business have we either on the left hand or the right hand of the Common Fool? The Common Fool, the born slave of stale tradition, suspicious, base and malignant, everlastingly bickering about out-of-date things. Our job is to emancipate him as much as we can, use him as well as we can and get rid of him as fast as we can."

"You use words with a greater boldness that I do," said Ratzel. "But you seem to be saying what I have in mind."

Catherine made a sudden observation. "I suppose it was necessary even for you to have this war before you could discover how little it was about."

Ratzel considered that. "I suppose it was."

"And now," said Catherine, "what are you going to do? What are you reasonable men who are so free from tradition and destiny, what are you going to do? How are you going to escape from the undying past? Which, I take it, is what the Common Fool is suffering from?"

"That's where our troubles begin. I doubt if over there I have twenty men with these ideas of ours fully expounded."

"I haven't a dozen."

Catherine went on like one who repeats an unfamiliar lesson.

"All the rest are asserting themselves in ways that you think evil – partial and disconnected anyhow – either pretending to be this or that but just playing for their own silly private hands, or really identifying themselves with some church, party, nation, some such *loyalty*" (she pronounced the word as though it stank) "no better than – how did you put it to me, Bolaris, once? – the cowardly aggressive identification of a cur with its house or pack. While *you?*"

"We also assert ourselves," said Bolaris.

"Living is self-assertion," said Ratzel to Catherine. "We also identify ourselves with something greater than ourselves. Only we flatter ourselves we have identified ourselves with something more final than any of these others. Something difficult to get beyond. That is our idea of ourselves. Maybe that isn't self-flattery. You believe, Bolaris, and I believe, in our hearts, that if a hard, clear-headed man carries his thought far enough he comes out where we are – and so by necessity joins us."

"That's only to believe ourselves sane."

"We two are self-assertive, as much fanatics, as much devotees, as any of the others. Yes. Every man is an assertion or a nonentity. We are not alone, brother Richard. The world swarms with our undiscovered brothers; elder brothers and younger brothers, big and little. An age of exposure. All the -ists and -isms of today are faint now with doubts and questions. Presently a multitude of our brothers will be turning up, but not perhaps so exactly under the same star as we."

"And sisters," said Catherine, and looked at Bolaris.

Bolaris met her eyes. He had an intense affection for her, an admiration, a belief in a sort of textural wisdom of body and impulse in her, far surpassing his own mental processes, and yet he had come reluctantly, as so many men come, to a profound disbelief in a woman's capacity for intellectual initiative. Maybe that was the price she paid for her unquestioning steadfastness to him. For a moment they scrutinized each other with an immense volume of unsaid mutual criticism behind their faintly smiling faces.

"Sisters," he said quietly.

"As you will," she said.

"And so to our stations," said Bolaris... "Well – good luck, Brother."

"Good luck."

They gripped hands and Bolaris said, "Stand up and look the damned prisoner you are."

He clapped his hands for the guards and the young officer and two men appeared and saluted.

5

Abruptly everything stood still. It was as if a motion picture suddenly ceased to turn over.

"*What's that?*"

Before Bolaris could give any directions a swift run of shots, crack, crack, crack, had come from the direction of the ravine. This whiff of firing brought everybody to rigid attention, and then as they stood and stared, silence closed upon them...

The picture began to move and talk again. Bolaris was the first to speak. "Could that have been Handon?" he said.

# CHAPTER SIX

## Pattern of a Horoscope

Everyone stood staring out of the great window at the distant woods and the sloping afternoon shadows upon the nearer masses of the converted convent. Two hospital attendants, small and remote, appeared on the parapet of the building and were followed by two soldiers who came and looked down towards the ravine, ducked and disappeared again. Bolaris made two steps towards the balcony and then turned to the young officer. "Take the prisoner downstairs," he said.

"What can be happening?" said Catherine stupidly.

"Keep back, my dear," said Bolaris, and went past her to the window.

Ratzel and his custodians marched into the passage.

From the broken country beyond the convent came the sound of a swift burst of machine-gun fire. Then suddenly at some point close at hand near the ravine an irregular crackle responded and there was a sound between a shout, a bark and a scream as if someone had been hit. Nothing was visible in the afternoon immobility. The olive trees and aloes, the rocks and the rose-tinted building against the blue mountain shapes, hung like a painted curtain in front of these noises.

Catherine saw Bolaris at the parapet of the balcony sniffing the air and moving his arm as though he was trying to grasp the form of the conflict that had sprung so suddenly out of the sweltering stillness of the afternoon. She went out towards him, but he motioned her back.

"Why should they try a raid now?" he asked, coming back into the room. "Can they know he's here? I thought they'd never dream we'd keep him here."

He sat down by the telephone.

He telephoned the Black Legion for support at once, explained the urgency of the situation to the commanding officer and then sent a man for the young subaltern. "Lock in your prisoner," he said, "and put every man you have at a window or out in the garden. We must hold the villa and leave the hospital to take care of itself. Bring in any men you have from the hospital. They'll respect the red cross if we've got no soldiers there. Look! someone is hoisting the flag. Good old Geneva!"

He made his disposition with an expert rapidity. He called up the Black Legion headquarters again to give further instructions. "Tumble to it," he said. His impression, he said, was that the Reds were in no great force and that a small detachment of the Black Legion with machine-guns should push up over the spur above the hospital, outflank the raiders and relieve the pressure on the villa. But they were to send down everyone they could.

Then he returned to the balcony. The firing he perceived was increasing and creeping nearer, along the ravine and towards the old convent wall. A bullet came smack against the cornice overhead and brought down a square yard of plaster.

"*Will* you go back?" he said to Catherine with affectionate exasperation.

There was a clatter from within the house and loud voices. Orders were being given by the young officer and brusque questions asked and answered.

2

Handon came headlong into the room clicking cartridges into his revolver. "Almost walked into it," he said. "Almost walked into it. They're all round us."

He saluted belatedly. "You ought to get away at once," he said. "They're three parts round us. The cars are under cover of the house – waiting. At any moment the attack may extend through those houses up beyond the hospital on the far side and block the road that way. There's nothing to hold them there. Nothing at all."

Handon was evidently hot, tired, surprised and confused in his mind. He had been running, he had been lying low, he had been crawling through wet red mud. His sweaty dirty skin, usually so fair, looked darker than the streak of ruddy hair across his forehead. He had been trying to think out a situation for himself. "They must have been coming over the hills all last night. There's no water, no supplies that way. Their own lines must be anything from a dozen to twenty miles away. They must know he is here. They must be coming for him – curse him!"

"But aren't there outposts up the slopes beyond the ravine?"

"They've come round them."

"They can't be in strength to get by like that."

"I don't think they are. Four or five companies perhaps. We were all among them before we knew. They never spotted us until we fired. I've been crawling back ever since. We'd have shot to warn you before, but they were coming along in parallel lines and they would have cut us off."

"The Black Legion won't get busy down here for another forty minutes," said Bolaris. "I don't like it. Shall we make a bolt? What have we got here?"

"A company and one or two details," said Handon, and Bolaris repeated his words. "Will you check that boy's arrangements, Handon. What ammunition has he and where's he put it?"

"You must bolt for it straight away," said Handon. "If you bolt at all. It's now or never."

Bolaris hesitated. He glanced at Catherine. He still had the Ratzel problem in mind. "See if we can hold out here first," he said, and Handon, after a doubtful glance at the two of them, went out of the room. He never liked leaving Bolaris with Catherine.

"If we bolt," said Bolaris. "Handon will insist on bringing Ratzel. That complicates everything. No. We stand a siege here. Far better. It can't last a half-hour. They seem to be easing off. Not a shot for the last three minutes. Hullo! *Glurrr!* That's one of their new magazine guns. Where was that?"

He returned to the balcony and surveyed the disposition of the defence. A rifle had been left out there and presently he picked it up, seemed disposed to take a shot with it at some unseen object and thought better of it. He came into the room, shrugged his shoulders and sat down.

"All our wonderful plans!" he said and laughed… "Anyhow he's out of the villa… He's away by now."

3

In five minutes Handon was back. "It's too late," he said; "the road's cut."

"No possibility of a dash?"

"They're quick workers. They've got some carts across the track. But they haven't come on. It's just sniping, that way. They can't be in force. I've given our chauffeurs guns and told them to lie out by the gates. But we ought to have thought about that before."

"Once a fight is started, Handon, the last thing you can do is to think. We were taken by surprise. How are our fellows behaving?"

"Quite well."

"We can hold it?"

"We have to."

"Still I'd like to hear more noise from the Black Legion. They ought to be out of their siesta now."

He went to the telephone and clicked at it.

"Damn!" he said.

"What?"

"The telephone's cut."

"Smart as well as quick. This was well planned."

"We've just got to stand a siege here until we're relieved. You'd better take over control, Handon."

Handon clanked out of the room shouting. "Hold to it, lads. There's relief coming. They thought they'd catch us napping."

Bolaris laughed and seemed elated, after his fashion when a situation tightened about him. He sat down in an easy chair. "Nothing I can do for a bit," he said.

He made a derisive gesture towards the door. "There'll be another shock for him presently," he remarked to Catherine.

He got up, decided not to look out of the window, smiled, shrugged his shoulders and sat down on the sofa beside Catherine. "It's all so absurdly unexpected," he said.

Her answer was drowned by a shot in the garden close at hand.

He made no movement towards the balcony. "No good popping out again," he said. "We don't want to draw their fire up here."

"But just now," she said. "Out there? You seemed to be going to shoot at someone?"

"I thought I saw a man down there in the gully. Then I thought better of it. It wasn't one of the attack. It was, you see, a man climbing down through the cactus bushes *away from us*."

"You think – ?"

"It was possible. I couldn't see very well because of the bushes."

"You mean he has escaped?"

"He is escaping now. And that's that."

He fell into thought. "Nothing to do," he said, "now, but to watch the turn of events. Funny if they do rush us and Ratzel gets me a prisoner on his hands! But I think Handon's soldier enough to stop that rush."

There were a few shots and then a lull in the firing.

The interval lengthened.

"Fantastic world," he said, "if we were not blind and prepossessed, we should see it as absurd as it is…

"Will he get away? Shall we ever make that peace? Shall we hold on until we can find our brothers – as he said?… Catherine, suddenly I doubt."

He might have been a hundred miles from any fighting, she thought. She stood looking down upon him.

"Will any human brotherhood ever get together, or is that all a dream? I know what I want with the world as clearly as ever I did, but suddenly something has taken away my confidence. Am I, after all, just a wilful dreamer of a world that can never arrive? Look at the world! Always the unexpected and a new twist to events... Will all the reason and desire in man be swept aside for ever by these incalculable slants? We plan. It is our nature to plan. But – but –

"Is this world really a reasonable world, Catherine, reasonable as the man of science supposes, or are the ruling patterns of life something quite different? Running right across all that we think rational – some perversity?

"If I had not met my brother again I should have been driving along quite a different line of ideas...

"Suppose, Catherine, that all this lot of pigeon-holes that we call words and reasoning, has just a chance fit upon reality – only fitting it so far and so much. Suppose – has it ever occurred to you, Catherine? that the real world – it must be orderly, it must be systematic. Yes – but that the real world has an irrational but elaborate order that diverges more and more from the order in our minds. A pattern that overlaps our minds for a time and then goes off in other directions. A pattern which we try to rationalize. And fail. Think how much that order has nonsense in it by any human standard. Look at butterflies' wings and sea-shells. Who can rationalize such patternings as that? Why are they – and how do they come? And if they are irrational and yet real, why should there not be other patternings – as irrational and as real? Why not horoscopes and twin destinies? That our fate should be written in the palms of our hands, and I and Ratzel live insanely linked!

"If that is so, Catherine, then all the views of life and its courses that we conceive, are no more than echoes made by the patterns in our eyes and brains. We are just prisms who sort out the rays of life in our way, bent mirrors that reflect them into relevant forms. Our minds are distorting mirrors and the wonderful worlds you see in them – ! Prisms and mirrors. That is all we are. Shatter the mirror and the story ends."

He laughed at her expression. "You think I'm talking nonsense," he said. "And for all practical purposes I am. We can't have it like that. We can't endure it like that. A day will come when we will have brought the hidden loveliness of a sunlit snow-crystal, drifting and melting on the other side of the moon a million years ago, into definite relation to the eternal human mind. Yes, and when the monstrous discrepancy between the scale of our lives and the starry intervals, will cease to be a disharmony. I don't know how such things can be achieved, but we shall achieve them. And then it will no longer seem necessary for men to be identical twins before they can think after the same fashion and work for a common end...

"But what's this uproar?"

His expression became alert. He clapped his hand to his revolver and stood up.


4


"He's gone. He's escaped!"

Handon was a breathless shouting fury in the room,

"Did they know he was here?... Do they know you are here? I ask you, how did they know it!... This raid!... Are we betrayed?... Has he been able to send messages to them? Treason. Treason I swear there is."

Bolaris stood beside Catherine.

"What has happened?"

"He's got down by a shaft as big as a cask that no one had the sense to stop. He's got away – God knows where. He's gone I tell you."

A ripple of fire grew to a volley. "There's the Black Legion coming into action up the village," said Bolaris.

Handon paid no heed to that. "For once I was right, I tell you, Chief – for once you have misjudged. You play with snakes and this is your reward. God knows who his allies were here. He must have had spies. God knows what the plotting has been... It is a planned escape. Somewhere now – In the drains and channels – "

He was struck by an idea. He went towards the balcony.

"Don't go there!" cried Bolaris.

Handon stared over his shoulder at his leader. "Why not?"

"You'll draw their fire."

Handon was out on the balcony and peering down. Then he was gesticulating. "He's there – *now!* That's Ratzel, creeping down among the agaves. By that olive tree."

Bolaris strode forward. "Leave him!" he cried. "Leave him alone!"

Handon was shouting, trying to attract the attention of some of the defenders below, and then suddenly he discovered there was a rifle against the parapet close at hand. Before Bolaris could reach him, he had raised it and fired. "*Got* him!" he said.

"Oh you fool!" cried Bolaris. "You accursed fool!" and leapt upon his right-hand man with murder in his eyes.

He gripped Handon's shoulder and snatched at the gun. Handon woke up to the fact that Bolaris was wrestling the rifle from his hands and for some inconceivable reason meant to kill him. There are limits to the loyalty even of a dog and Handon resisted.

They struggled for two seconds while the woman stood paralysed, and then the rifle cracked again and Bolaris was spinning back with a neat hole drilled through his body and through his heart. He fell at Catherine's feet with blood pouring from his mouth and spurting from his back, and she dropped on her knees beside him, regardless of the stupefied Handon who stood, gun in hand, staring at his dying chief.

"I've shot *him!*" he cried. "*Him!* I didn't mean it. How could I have meant it? It caught against my belt."

Catherine took no notice of him. She was staring with a stunned expression at the face of her lover. His mouth was open half-way between a smile and a laugh and a broad band of blood widened from the lower corner. The life had vanished from his eyes.

Handon bent down over her, his dirty face distorted with grief. He was trying to say something that she would not heed. "I loved him, I tell you – more than you did."

He found her inexpressiveness unendurable. He discovered the rifle in his hand and flung it across the room. Then he strode after it, picked it up and rushed out.

Only slowly did Catherine's mind revive.

With a sound like tearing cloth a bullet came flying into the room and a mirror with a frame of cut-glass flew into a cloud of sparkling dust.

Her eyes went to the broken fragments of glass that rolled and slid and spread and scattered on the floor. It was as if they were explaining something. Until they ceased to move.

"Prisms and mirrors," she whispered. "Our picture vanishes as the mirror breaks! You were saying that, darling. Five minutes ago you were saying that.

"Speak to me…

"No. The pattern of your life! Over. And mine. And all the fine things that seemed beginning…

"Dreams about brotherhood…meaning as little as the pattern on a sea-shell."

Outside the guns rattled and then came a shout of "Let them have it!" and the groans, screams, retchings, rendings and curses of a sudden bayonet fight in the garden beneath the window.

She listened for a time to those hideous noises.

"No," she whispered to the still face close to hers. "It cannot end like this. We were just the first. We were just the beginning. It was a beginning…"

She whispered still lower with her mouth awry: "Say it *was* a beginning, my dear. Speak to me, speak just once again.

"Tell me what am I to do…"

# The Croquet Player

To Moura

# CHAPTER ONE

## The Croquet Player

I have been talking to two very queer individuals and they have produced a peculiar disturbance of my mind. It is hardly an exaggeration to say that they have infected me and distressed me with some very strange and unpleasant ideas. I want to set down what it is they have said to me, in the first place for my own sake, so as to clear up my thoughts about it. What they told me was fantastic and unreasonable, but I shall feel surer about that if I set it down in writing. Moreover I want to get my story into a shape that will enable one or two sympathetic readers to reassure me about the purely imaginative quality of what these two men had to say.

It is a sort of ghost story they unfolded. But it is not an ordinary ghost story. It is much more realistic and haunting and disturbing than any ordinary ghost story. It is not a story of a haunted house or a haunted churchyard or anything so limited. The ghost they told me about was something much larger than that, a haunting of a whole countryside, something that began as an uneasiness and grew into a fear and became by slow degrees a spreading presence. And still it grew – in size, in power and intensity. Until it became a continual overshadowing dread. I do

103

not like this ghost that grows and spreads, even although it does so only in the mind. But I had better begin at the beginning and tell about this story as far as I can, and the manner in which it came to me.

But first I had better give a few particulars about myself. Of course I would rather I did not, but I doubt if you will realize my position without it. I am probably one of the best croquet players alive, and that I am not a bit ashamed of saying. I am also a first-rate archer. One is neither of these things without a considerable amount of discipline and balance in one's make-up. Many people, I know, find me a trifle effeminate and ridiculous because I make croquet my game; they say as much behind my back and at times they betray it to my face, and I admit there have been moments when I have been inclined to agree with them. But on the other hand quite a lot of people seem to like me, everybody calls me Georgie in an affectionate manner, and on the whole I am inclined to like myself. It takes all sorts to make a world, and I see no sense in pretending to be the human norm when one is not. Regarded from a certain angle I am no doubt a soft, but all the same I can keep my head and temper at croquet and make a wooden ball perform like a trained animal. Even at tennis I can make some of the fiercer sort extremely cross and silly. And I can do sleight-of-hand tricks, for which you certainly need nerve and complete self-possession, as well as most professionals.

As a matter of fact a lot of these tremendous sporting people, record breakers, gamblers and so on are much more akin to me than they like to think. There is a lot of sham in their pretension to hairiness and virility. At heart they are as tame as I am. They have chosen to be boxed up in games. I suppose cricket and hockey and so on are more gladiatorial than my sort of sport, aviation and motoring more lethal and gambling more vexatious, but I do not see there is any greater reality in what they do than in what I do. Risk is not reality. They are players just as I am a player. They are enclosed with me in the same pleasant round of harmless and fruitful activities.

I admit I have had an exceptionally uneventful life. I missed the experience of the Great War by a couple of years, and my life has always been an extremely sheltered and comfortable one. I was brought up by my paternal aunt, Miss Frobisher, *the* Miss Frobisher of the Barton Chapel Case and the Woman's World Humanity Movement, and it is only slowly that I have come to realize that my upbringing was – if I may be paradoxical – unusually banal. I have led a life largely of negatives and avoidances. I have been trained to keep calm and civil and not react excitedly to surprises. And above all to regard only ordinary decent everyday things seriously.

My aunt took me over at the age of three when my parents divorced, and since then she has never let go of me. She is a woman with what, to be frank, one might call a natural hostility to sexual facts, and my parents' misbehaviour – those were the days when the papers published full reports of divorce cases – and some of the details of the affair shocked her extremely. When I went to school at Harton, she took a house close by and entered me as a day-boy, and she did practically the same thing while I was at Keble. Possibly I am naturally just a little inclined to be what the Americans call a sissy, and this tendency has been favoured by these circumstances.

I have soft hands and an ineffective will. I prefer not to make important decisions. My aunt has trained me to be her constant associate and, with displays and declarations on all possible occasions of an immense maternal passion for me, she has – I know it clearly – made me self-indulgent and dependent. Yet I do not blame her very much or resent it very much. It is how we two have been made. She has always been rich and free to do as she liked not only with herself but with others, and I have always felt well-off and secure. Our lives have been easy so far. Like most well-born, well-off people, we have taken inferiors for granted, servants for granted, and the general good behaviour of the world towards us. I suppose there are still hundreds of thousands of people in the world as sure of all the material best of life as we are and taking it in the same matter-of-course fashion.

"What shall we do?" we ask. "Where shall we go?" Nobody compels us. We are the floating cream of humanity.

We have a house in Upper Beamish Street, a modest little place in Hampshire, and we move about a lot. My aunt, as many people know, is a very temperamental woman – I do not mean temperamental in any unpleasant sense – and sometimes we are as keen as mustard on this Woman's World Humanity Movement – though I have never clearly understood what it is all about – travelling over the world for it – so far, that is, as there are bathrooms *en suite*, upon which my aunt insists – "making contacts", usually until there is a difficulty over the committee election or something of that sort and my aunt gets disgusted, and then for a year or so we drop Woman's World Humanity and go round wiping up the lawns with croquet champions or winning tassels with our archery. We are both quite extraordinarily good at the long-bow, and my aunt has been painted as Diana by Wilmerdings. But croquet is our especial gift. If we did not shrink from the publicity and vulgarity of it we could certainly be champions. We also play a pretty decent tennis game, and our golf might easily be worse, but the popular criticism of tennis has been carried to such high levels that we do not care to be seen playing, and golf we find mixes us up with all sorts of people. Sometimes we just recuperate. Lately we have been recuperating at Les Noupets after a rather discouraging conference of the Woman's World Humanity Movement at Chicago. (The less said about those American delegates the better, but my aunt was fully equal to them.)

That, I think, is a quite sufficient explanation of myself and my atmosphere. The two club lawns at Les Noupets were excellent and we found an admirable secretary-typist who dealt with my aunt's very extensive correspondence about the movement and particularly with her libel case against Mrs Glyco-Harriman, taking it all down in shorthand, typing it in the afternoon and bringing it for revision after tea. There were one or two sets of niceish people with whom a little light conversation was possible without entanglement. Croquet an hour before lunch and perhaps in the afternoon again and dinner at eight. We never play bridge until after dinner; it is our inflexible rule. So that I had a certain amount of time upon my hands while she wrote what would be in the case of anyone without her provocation extremely abusive as well as sarcastic letters, which I devoted chiefly to a morning's walk up the hill to the Perona springs, where I took the waters, rather for fun than with any idea of a cure, and then sat in a state of wholesome idleness on the terrace of the Source hotel removing the inky taste by appropriately chosen refreshment. My aunt is inclined to a non-alcoholic attitude, but of late years I have found the unobtrusive exercise of my private judgment in such matters not only permissible but better for both of us. I mean I am a more cheerful companion.

I think all that gets me fairly well, and now with your permission I will put myself into the background, so to speak – or "frame" perhaps is better – and tell you about the first of these two queer men I met on the Perona terrace.

# CHAPTER TWO

## The Haunting Fear in Cainsmarsh

It was while I was sitting out on the terrace in the sun, nibbling a brioche and consuming a harmless Vermouth and Seltzer, that I first set eyes on Dr Finchatton. He was two tables away, and he was having an almost violent quarrel with a number of books he had got from the Les Noupets tea-shop and lending library. He was opening them one after another, reading a few pages, turning them over, muttering and banging them down on the ground with an emphasis that would have distressed the library people extremely. He looked up and caught my reproving eye. He stared and then smiled.

"Scores of books," he said; "hundreds of books – and not one worth reading! They're all – *off* it."

There was something comical and irrational about his disgust that amused me. "Then why read them?" I asked. "Reading crowds the memory and prevents one thinking."

"Exactly what I want to do. I came over here to stop thinking – and forget. And I can't." His voice which to begin with was clear and distinct rose to an angry note. "Some of these books bore – some irritate. Some even remind me of just what I am trying to forget."

Stepping over his heap of condemned volumes he came, glass and carafe in hand, and without any invitation from me sat down at the table beside me. He looked me in the face with an expression that was at once friendly and slightly quizzical. I know my face is – well, "cherubic" – for a man of thirty-three, and it was very evident he appreciated the fact. "Do *you* do much thinking?" he asked.

"A fair amount. I solve *The Times* Cross-Word Puzzle nearly every day. I play a lot of chess – by correspondence chiefly. And I'm not so bad at bridge."

"I mean real thinking. About things that pursue and worry you and cannot be explained."

"I don't let things worry me," I said.

"Do you happen to be interested in ghosts – and hauntings?"

"I'm neutral. I don't believe in ghosts, but I don't *dis*believe in them. If you follow me. I've never seen a ghost. I think there is a lot to be said for spiritualism, quite a lot, in spite of much imposture. I suppose immortality has been proved, now, by that sort of thing, and that is all to the good. My aunt Miss Frobisher is quite of that opinion. But I feel that the necessary table-rapping and cabinet seances and all that is a job for a specialist."

"But suppose you found there were ghosts all about you?"

"I never have."

"And there's nothing – here for instance – that makes you feel uneasy?"

"Where?" I asked.

"*There*," he said and waved a hand at the tranquil sea and the innocent sky.

"Why should there be?"

"But *is* there?"

110

"No."

"I envy your insensitiveness – or your imperturbability." He emptied his glass and ordered another half litre of wine. Either out of ignorance or preference he was drinking red ordinaire. "*You* don't feel there is anything? No danger?"

"I never saw a more tranquillizing view. Not a cloud."

"It isn't so with me... I've had some very disturbing experiences. I'm still disturbed. Curious! You feel nothing. Maybe it's just the aftermath of what has happened."

"What *has* happened? And what is the aftermath?"

"I'd like to tell you," he said. "It's rather a yarn, you know."

"Go ahead," said I.

And with that much introduction he began to tell me his story. He was rather disconnected at first and then he settled down to it. He told it to me not as though he particularly wished to tell it to me, but as though he wanted very badly to tell it to someone and hear how it sounded. After he had got started I interrupted very little.

It was indiscreet of me perhaps to let him begin upon me. I knew nothing of him. I had to ask him for his name before he named himself. Evidently he was queer in some way – I should have remembered that the big house above the town was supposed to be a "Home" for mental cases, a psycho-therapeutic institution as they call them nowadays, and the discreet thing for me would have been to have sheered off there and then upon some excuse before his story began.

Yet there was nothing about him to warn me off him. There was nothing eccentric in his manner or indeed in his general appearance. He had the jaded look of a man who doesn't sleep well, a little dark under the eyes, but apart from that he seemed quite all right. He was quietly dressed in the Englishman's usual grey, he wore a coloured shirt and an unobtrusive tie. It was a little askew but that was nothing. Plenty of men never put on their ties straight – though how they can stand it I can't think. It is so easy to get a tie straight. He was decidedly lean and fairly good-looking, with what I suppose one would call a sensitive mouth below his short moustache. He leant forward most of the time with his arms folded under his chest much as a cat folds up its paws. He talked perhaps just a little on the emphatic side but he seemed on the watch to control himself. And as I had a full hour or more to dispose of before I went down Les Noupets again, I let him run on, without any attempt to interrupt him or cut him short.

"At first," he said, "I thought it was the marshes."

"What marshes?"

"Cainsmarsh. You have heard of Cainsmarsh?"

I used to be pretty good at geography at school but I could not recall that name. But I did not like to admit my ignorance on the spur of the moment. Something about the word seemed familiar. "Marsh" seemed a clue. Vague suggestions of fenny country, watery expanses, a lowering sky, dank black thatch, moored old barges and the hum of mosquitoes floated across my mind.

"A great district for malaria and rheumatic complaints," he said, confirming my impression. "I bought a practice there... Forgive a touch of autobiography. I did so partly because it was an exceptionally cheap practice and I had to earn a living somehow with my small resources, and partly because I wanted to leave the Hospital and London – and rest my brain. I went there jaded and disappointed. It seemed likely to be an easy-going job. There is practically no competition in the marshes, not until you get towards the part they call the Island, where the market-town doctors come out in their cars. The parishes up towards the hills such as they are and out towards the saltings are quite beyond their range except for special consultations. I had to go into practice with a minor qualification because of the need I was under for tranquillizing surroundings... I threw up the prospect of a medical degree."

He paused as though he found a difficulty.

"Were you ill?" I enquired, to help him out. "Why *did* you leave the hospital with a minor qualification? Forgive me making a personal remark, but you don't look the sort of man who muffs exams."

"I didn't muff exams. In fact I was more than usually ambitious. I worked, I think, too hard. And I was active mentally in other directions. I was keener on politics than most medical students. And I got very keen on social justice and the prevention of war. Very keen on the war question. I had been working on gas. Perhaps I *did* too much. Perhaps I thought and felt too much... Yes... Yes, certainly I felt too much. A time came when the morning paper could upset me so as to spoil my work for the day.

"From the very beginning of my medical education, you must know, I found myself under a strain. I admit that. I didn't like dissection; I didn't like the damaged human stuff in the wards. Some of it was pitiful; some of it horrified me."

I agreed with him. "Doctoring has always terrified *me. I* couldn't stand any of it."

"But the world must have doctors," he said.

"It won't have *me* for a doctor. I've never seen more than three dead people, and they were all lying quietly laid out in bed."

"But on the road? You come upon dreadful sights."

"We never travel by road. All sane people are giving it up."

"You, I see, have avoided the ugly side of life from the first. Well, – I didn't. I walked right into it when I chose medicine. I thought of the good I could do and I never thought of the harsh red realities I should have to face. You avoided. I tried not to avoid and then I ran away. I went to that district with the full idea of escape. This, I told myself, will be away from any war there is or any bombing. Here I can recover myself. Here, I said, there will be nothing except normal cases I can really face and help. Cainsmarsh is far from any main roads. There won't be even motor casualties, which are often so frightful to encounter. You see my point? It looked as good as any possible world for me, and going there in summer-time with the wild flowers out and a hundred sorts of butterfly about, dragon-flies and an abundance of summer birds, let alone a lot of summer visitors, mostly houseboat and fishing people with children and their small ailments, there didn't seem to be very much wrong with it. I would have laughed if you had told me that I had come into a haunted land.

"I did all I could to protect myself from over-stimulation. I did not have a newspaper in the house. I relied on a weekly news summary with no illustrations but diagrams. I wouldn't open a book later than Dickens.

"The native population seemed at first just a trifle stupid and reserved but quite kindly. I saw nothing wrong with them to begin with. Old Rawdon, the vicar of Cross in Slackness, that landmark church of the levels, told me that there was a good deal of furtive drugging because of the ague and that he suspected the genuineness of their amiability. I went to pay my respects to him as soon as I was able. He was an elderly man and rather deaf, and he had exchanged to the Cross in Slackness living because of his infirmity. His church and vicarage were stranded, so to speak, with one or two cottages on a sort of crocodile back of land and they were overgrown with elm trees. I doubt if even as many as a score of people came to his services. He was not very communicative, his old bent wife was even less so, he had trouble with gall-stones and an ulcerated contusion of the ankle and his chief preoccupation seemed to be with the high-church tendencies of his fellow priest, a newly arrived curate at Marsh Havering. Apparently he himself was low church and Calvinistic, but at first I could not understand the mixture of fear and resentment with which he spoke of the younger man. There were no landed gentry in Cainsmarsh, and, except for a veterinary surgeon, a few elementary teachers, one or two publicans and some middle-class boarding-house keepers towards Beacon Ness, the population was entirely a population of farmers and farm workers. They had no folk-lore, no songs, no arts and no special costume. A more improbable soil for anything you could call psychic it would be hard to imagine. And yet you know – "

He frowned and spoke in measured words, as if he was doing his utmost to be explicit and was reasoning against the possible objections I might presently make to what he had to tell me.

"After all – It is in just such a flat, still atmosphere perhaps – translucent, gentle coloured, that things lying below the surface, things altogether hidden in more eventful and colourful surroundings, creep on our perceptions…"

He paused, drank a glass of his wine, reflected for a moment and resumed.

115

"There can be no disputing the stillness of that district. Sometimes I would stop my car on one of the winding dyke roads and stand listening before I went on again. One would hear the sheep upon the lavender-coloured hills, four or five miles away, or the scream of some distant water-fowl, like a long, harsh scratch of neon light across the silent blue, or the sound of the wind and the sea, a dozen miles away at Beacon Ness, like the world breathing in its sleep. At night of course there were more noises: dogs howled and barked in the distance, corncrakes called and things rustled in the reeds. And yet the nights too could sometimes have a stillness...

"At first it did not seem to be of any particular significance that the traceable consumption of soporifics and opiates by this apparently insensitive population was not only quite remarkably high but increasing, nor that the proportion of suicides and inexplicable crimes – inexplicable as distinguished from normally motivated offences – over this part of the world was exceptional and apparently rising. Dealing with such a small population, however, a murder more or less could upset the percentage altogether. Face to face in the daylight there was nothing at all murderous in the bearing of these people. They did not look you in the eye – but that may have been their idea of good manners. It just happened that there had been no less than three crazy murders of relations and neighbours in Cainsmarsh in the past five years, and of two of them the perpetrators were still undiscovered. The other was a fratricide. The vicar when I spoke about this said something about 'degenerate race – too inbred' and changed the subject, as though it was an unpleasant topic of no particular importance for him.

"The first real intimation I had in my own person of the brooding strangeness that hangs over Cainsmarsh was an attack of insomnia. Hitherto I had been a fairly sound sleeper, but before I had settled in the marsh for a couple of months my nights began to be troubled. I would wake up in a state of profound uneasiness, and without any physiological cause that I could trace I fell a prey to evil dreams. They were quite peculiar dreams, like none I had ever dreamt before. They were dreams of menace, of being waylaid, stalked and pursued and of furious struggles to defend myself, dreams out of which I would wake shouting – you know those faint, shadowy shouts of dreamland conflicts – sweating and trembling in every limb. Some of these dreams had so strong a flavour of horror that they would leave me afraid to go to sleep again. I would try to read, and whatever I read in the night watches an eerie discomfort hung over me.

"I adopted all the expedients that would naturally occur to a young medical man to end these enervating experiences, but without avail. I dieted. I exercised. I would get up and dress, go out either on foot or in my car, in spite of a strong fear resistance. Fear pursued me out of those dreams. The nightmare quality hung about me and could not be shaken off. I was awake and still dreaming. Never have I seen such sinister skies as I did on those night excursions. I felt such a dread of unfamiliar shadows as I had not known even in childhood. There were times on those nocturnal drives when I could have shouted aloud for daylight as a man suffocating in a closed chamber might shout for air.

"Very naturally this inability to sleep began presently to undermine my daily life. I became nervous and fanciful. I found I was giving way to minor hallucinations, rather, I suppose, after the pattern of delirium tremens. But with more menace in them.

I would turn convulsively under the impression that a silent hound was creeping up to attack me from behind, or I would imagine a black snake wriggling out from under the valance of an armchair.

"Presently came other symptoms of relaxing mental control. I found myself suspecting the Island doctors of a combination against me. The most petty incidents, small slights, breaches of etiquette, fancied imputations had been seized upon by my imagination and worked up into the fabric of a conspiracy mania. I had to restrain myself from writing foolish letters or making challenges and asking questions. Then I began to find something evil in the silence or in the gestures of some of my patients. And while I sat by their bedsides I fancied that there were hostile goings-to-and-fro and malignant whisperings and conspirings just outside the door.

"I could not understand what was the matter with me. I searched my mind for nervous stresses and I could find none. I had surely left all that behind in London. Temperature and so forth remained normal. But clearly there was something askew in my adjustment to these new surroundings. Cainsmarsh was disappointing my expectations. There was no healing in it for me. I had to pull myself together. I had sunk all my little capital in the practice and I had to stick it. There was nowhere else for me to go. I had to keep my head and grapple with this trouble and beat it before it became too much for me.

"Was it just my own trouble? Was something specially wrong with me or was it something wrong with the countryside? Were there other people in the Marsh having dreams and fancies like mine, or maybe was this a trouble that came to newcomers and passed away? Was it something I should get over? A sort of acclimatization. I had to be careful with my enquiries because it is not well for a doctor to admit he is out of sorts. I began to watch my patients, my old servant and anyone with whom I came in contact for any betrayal of symptoms similar to mine. And I found what I looked for. Beneath the superficial stolidity a number of these people were profoundly uneasy. There was fear in the Marsh for them as for me. It was an established habitual fear. But it was not a definite fear. They feared something unknown. It was a sort of fear that might concentrate at any time upon anything whatever and transform it into a thing of terror.

"Let me give you some instances.

"One evening I found an old lady stiff with dread at a shadow in a corner, and when I moved her candle and the shadow moved, she screamed aloud. 'But it can't hurt you,' I argued. 'I'm afraid,' she answered, as though that was a sufficient answer. And suddenly before I could prevent her she had seized a little clock on the night-table beside her and flung it at that dark and dreadful nothingness, and buried her head under the clothes. I will confess that for a moment or so I stood rigid and expectant staring at the broken clock in the corner.

"And one day I saw a farmer who was rabbit-shooting pause, stare aghast at a fluttering scarecrow and then, unaware of my presence, suddenly raise his gun and blow the poor dangling old rapscallion to bits.

"There was an unusual terror of the dark. My old servant, I found, would not venture out after twilight to the pillar-box a hundred yards away. She would make every sort of excuse and when she was cornered she refused absolutely to go. I had to go myself or leave my letters until the morning. Even sweethearting,

I learnt, would not tempt the young people abroad after sundown.

"I can't tell you," he said, "how the perception of the presence of fear grew upon me and grew upon me – how it infected me – until at last the flap of a window-blind in the breeze or the fall of a cinder in the fireplace would set my nerves aquiver.

"I could not shake this off; my nights got worse. I determined to have a real talk about this queer uneasiness of the mind with the old vicar. In his way, you see, the district was his business, as in my way it was mine. He ought to know whatever was to be known. By this time the disorder was getting a strong hold upon me. I made up my mind to go to him after a night of exceptional horror and dismay. I was indeed already pretty bad...

"I can recall here and now the unprotected feeling of my drive to him across the open marshes. They seemed to me far too open, bare to endless dangers. And yet when I came near a clump of trees or bushes it took on the quality of an ambush. The normal confidence of a living creature was deserting me. I felt not simply exposed to incalculable evils, I felt threatened by them. In broad daylight, mind you; in the sunshine. With nothing but a few birds in sight...

"As it happened I caught the old man in a communicative mood. I put my questions plainly to him. 'I'm a newcomer in this country,' I said. 'Is there something – something *peculiarly* wrong about it?'

"He stared at me and scratched his cheek, weighing what he should tell me. 'Yes,' he said, 'there is.'

"He led me into his study, listened for a moment as if to make sure that everyone was out of earshot and then closed the door carefully. 'You're sensitive,' he said. 'You're getting it sooner than I did. Something – wrong – wrong and getting worse. Something evil.'

"I remember those opening words very plainly and his bleary old eyes and the bad teeth in his sagging mouth. He came and sat down quite close to me, with one long bony hand cupping his hairy ear. 'Don't speak too loud,' he said. 'If you speak distinctly I can hear.'

"He said he was glad to have someone to talk it over with at last. He told me how he had hoped to end his days in the Marsh quietly, and how gradually this shadowy discomfort had come over him, deepening slowly into fear. He could never afford another exchange. He too was fixed. It was hard to talk about. His wife would never talk to him about it. Before they came to Cross in Slackness, they had been the best of friends and gossips. 'Now,' he said, 'it is pushing us apart. I have to talk to myself. I don't know what's come over her.'

"What is pushing you apart?" I asked.

" 'The Evil.'

"That was his name for it.

"Everyone, he said, was being pushed apart. You began to find sinister possibilities in the most ordinary relations. Lately he had had a curious suspicion of his food – had fancied a queer taste in it and queer feelings after it. 'It makes me fear for my reason,' he said. 'My reason or hers.' Yet all the same, it was queer about the food. Why should anyone – ? He left it at that. At his first coming the common people had seemed simply dull to him. Then he had begun to realize that they were not so much dull as reserved and suspicious. You would catch a glance in their eyes like a dog that may snap. Even the children when you came to watch them were furtively defensive. For no reason. For no reason at all. He told me that, sitting very close to me, not speaking too loud.

"He came closer. 'They are cruel to animals,' he told me. 'They beat their dogs and horses. Not regularly. By fits.'

" 'The children come to school with marks on them,' he said… 'You can't get them to say anything… They are afraid.'

"I asked him if he felt that this thing, whatever it was, was increasing. Had it always been there? There was very little recorded history of the region. He thought it was increasing. Things had not always been like this. I suggested that it may have always been in the atmosphere of the place and that we became more aware of it as we fell under the spell.

" 'Maybe. Partly that,' said the old vicar.

"He gave some broken fragments of a story about a former incumbent. He and his wife had been sent to prison for cruelty to a servant girl. Prison! They said she told lies and had dirty habits. As an excuse. They wanted to cure her, they said. But really they just hated her… Never anything against them before they came into the Marsh.

" 'It's always been here,' whispered the old vicar. 'Always. Below the surface. An unhappy, wicked spirit that creeps into us all. I pray. I do not know what would happen to me if I did not pray. What with the waste of money and the rudeness of everybody and the malicious mischief they do me and the stone-throwing. Let alone the poison. It is the poisoning hurts me most.'

"We talked like that in his big, shabby, sparely furnished study in the broad daylight, like men who cower in a cave.

"And then he began to talk less sanely. The evil was in the soil, he declared, *underground*. He laid great stress on the word

122

'underground'. He made a downward gesture with his quivering hand. There was something mighty and dreadful buried in Cainsmarsh. Something colossally evil. Broken up. Scattered all over the Marsh. 'I think I know what it is,' he whispered darkly, but for a time he would not explain.

"They kept on stirring it up, he said; they would not let it rest.

"Whom did he mean by *they?* That was difficult. There had been road-making, there had been drainage works and now 'those archaeologists'! And that was not all. There had been a ploughing of old pastures during the war. Opening old sores. 'You see over all the place was once a wilderness of graves.'

"Tumuli?" I questioned.

" 'No,' he insisted, 'Graves – graves everywhere!' And some of the ancient people, he said, were 'petrified'. You found stones of the strangest shapes. Abominable shapes. 'They keep on bringing things up,' he said. 'Things that had better be left alone. Ought to be let alone. Making doubts and puzzles – destroying faith.'

"At a jump he was denouncing Darwinism and evolution. It was remarkable how life-long controversies had interwoven with his Cainsmarsh distresses! Had I seen the museum at Eastfolk? he asked.

"He talked of the great bones exhibited there. But I protested he was thinking of the bones of mammoths and dinosaurs and suchlike things. Giants, he insisted. Look at what they call implements there! Too big and clumsy for any living man to handle. Axes, spears – nothing but huge weapons for killing and killing! *'Murder stones'* he called them. The murder stones of giants.

"He clenched his bony fist, his quavering voice rose and real hatred came into his eyes.

" 'Nothing is too bad,' he said, 'for the men who dig up those bones. Tearing up dark secrets. Seeming to confute... A grave's a grave and a dead man's a dead man, even if he's been dead a million years. Let the evil creatures lie! Let them lie! Let their dust lie!' He ceased to be furtively confidential; his anger rose and thrust his fear aside. He no longer troubled to listen to anything I had to say in reply to him.

"He was soon launched upon the wildest diatribe. He was transfigured by an anger that shook his feeble frame. He had fixed upon the local archaeologists and naturalists as the chief objective for his tirade, but mixed up with that in the oddest and most illogical way was his detestation of the high church practices that had been introduced by the new man at Marsh Havering. Just when this Evil was being released and rising like an exhalation from the earth, when the one supreme need of the time was religion straight and stern – '*straight and stern*' he repeated and shook his fingers in my face – this man must come with his vestments and images and music and mummery!

"But I will not give you, if I could, an imitation of that poor old wreck as he grew fiercer and louder and hoarser. He wanted suppression, he wanted persecution, of Science, of Rome, of every sort of immorality and immodesty, of every sort of creed except his own, persecution, enforced repentance, to save us from the Wrath that was coming steadily upon us. 'They turn up the soil, they strip things bare, and we breathe the dust of long dead men.' It was as if he was trying to escape from our common marshland obsession by sheer screaming violence. 'The doom of Cain!' he shouted. 'The punishment of Cain!'

" 'But *why* Cain?' I managed to insert.

" 'He ended his days here,' the old man declared. 'Oh I know! Is this called Cainsmarsh for nothing? He wandered over the face of the earth and at last he came here, he and the worst of his sons. They poisoned the earth. Age after age of crime and cruelty, and then the Flood buried them under these marshes – and there they ought to be buried for ever.'

"I tried to argue against this fantasy – Cainsmarsh is just a corruption of Gaynes Marsh, as all the guide-books say; it is written Gaynes in Domesday Book – but the old man bore me down. My voice had no chance now amidst his croaking assertions. His deafness was a shield against all argument. His voice filled the room. He poured out the festering accumulations of his brooding solitude. His sentences had the readiness of long-matured expression. I guess most of it had been uttered, time and again, to the faithful remnant of Cross in Slackness church. He had got the children of Cain and the cave-men and the mammoths and megatheria and dinosaurs all jumbled up in the wildest confusion. It was a storm of preposterous nonsense. And yet – And yet, you know – "

Dr Finchatton regarded the bay of Les Noupets in silence for a few moments.

"Out of it all came a suggestion. I doubt if it will seem even remotely sane to you – in this clear air. But it was the suggestion that this haunting something was something remote, archaic, bestial…"

He nodded his head in doubtful confirmation of what he was saying.

"You see… It's bad enough to be haunted by Georgian ghosts, Stuart ghosts, Elizabethan ghosts, ghosts in armour and ghosts in chains. Yet anyhow, one has a sort of fellow feeling for them. They aren't just spirits of cruelty, suspicion and ape-like malice. But the souls of a tribe of cave-men might be... Grisly ghosts... What do *you* think?"

"One may be as possible as the other," I said.

"Yes. And yet, if cave-men, why not apes? Suppose all our ancestors rose against us! Reptiles, fish, amoebae! The idea was so fantastic that as I drove away from Cross in Slackness I tried to laugh."

Dr Finchatton stopped short and looked at me.

"*I couldn't laugh*," he said.

"I don't think *I* could have done," I said. "It's a frightful idea. I'd rather be haunted by a man than an ape any day."

"I drove back home more saturated with terror than I came. I was beginning to see visions now everywhere. There was an old man bending down in a ditch doing something to a fallen sheep and he became a hunched, bent and heavy-jawed savage. I did not dare look to see what he was doing, and when he called something to me – maybe only a good-day-to-you – I pretended not to hear. Whenever a clump of bushes came near the road my heart sank and I slackened pace and as soon as I was past I jammed down the accelerator.

"I got drunk, sir, for the first time in my life that night. You see, it was either getting drunk or running away. Maybe I'm still a young doctor, but that's my code. A doctor who quits his practice without notice is as bad as a sentinel who bolts. So you see, I had to get drunk.

"Before I went to bed I found I was funking opening the front door to look out. So with a convulsive effort I flung it open wide...

"There crouched the marshes under the moonlight and the long low mists seemed to have stayed their drifting at the slam of the door against the wall. As if they paused to listen. And over it all was something, a malignant presence such as I had never apprehended before.

"Nevertheless I stuck to my doorstep. I did not retreat. I attempted even a drunken speech.

"I forget what I said. Maybe I myself went far enough back to the Stone Age to make mere inarticulate sounds. But the purport was defiance – of every evil legacy the past has left for man."

# CHAPTER THREE

## The Skull in the Museum

At this point in his narrative Dr Finchatton stopped abruptly. "This sounds a crazy story to you?" he said. "Do you want me to go on with it?"

"Not in the least," I spluttered. "I mean yes, please. I mean, do *please* go on. I'm tremendously interested. But sitting here at this table with everything bright and clear and definite, there is a certain unreality – if you understand me?"

"*I* understand you," he said without returning my smile. He looked round. "It does seem here as though nothing except vermouth and seltzer and lunch-time presently, and things like that, could ever happen any more."

A look of extreme weariness came over him. "I'm resting," he said. "Yes. But sooner or later I shall have to go back to it all. I'd like to go on talking about it a bit – to you. If you don't mind. There's something – if I might say so – so refreshingly unimaginative about you. Like white paper."

At the time I was quite prepared to go on listening. I was oblivious then of the possibility that this story might ever disturb my own slumbers. I keep dreams for waking moments but I like them then. Fancies and reveries. I welcome them. One dreams

129

then but one feels quite safe. There may be shivers in it but no real fear. It is just because they *are* impossible that I like impossible stories. Ever since I discovered Edgar Allan Poe in my early boyhood I have had a taste for the weird and the eerie, and in spite of my aunt's opposition – she flies into a regular passion at the suggestion that anything irregular or unusual can ever occur – I have – in an unobtrusive way – indulged it pretty freely. Her imagination, I think, was killed long ago, but mine I've made into a domestic pet that I like to play with. I do not think it will ever claw me seriously; it's a pussy now which knows where to stop. Though I am not so sure of that as I was. But it was very pleasant to be there, safe and solid, in the clear Normandy sunshine, and hear about those terror-stricken marshes. "Go on, my dear sir," said I. "Go on."

"Well," said Dr Finchatton, "I put up as much fight as my training and quality permitted. Getting drunk and that speech of defiance, even if in fact I imagined it rather than made it, did me good. I slept that night, good forgetful sleep, for the first time for weeks, and next day rose refreshed to reckon with my situation. Trained as I was, it was natural for me to assume that this common ailment of fear and fantasy, this sickness of a whole region, must be due to some virus in the air or the water or the soil. I made a private resolution to drink water only after it had been boiled and eat only well-cooked food. But also I was quite open to the idea that something less material might be at work. I am no prejudiced materialist. I was quite prepared to believe in purely psychic infection – though not of course in these Sons of Cain of the vicar's. I decided next morning that I would investigate that High-Church curate at Marsh Havering, the

Reverend Mortover, the object of the vicar's peculiar detestation, and find what *he* might have to say about it.

"But I found the young man as mad as his Calvinistic colleague. If the old man mixed the trouble up with science and excavations and Romanism, the young man blamed the Reformation and made great play with the Puritan witch mania of the sixteenth century. Some spiritual control was broken then, he assured me with the utmost confidence. Diabolism had returned to the earth. It was not the ghost of Cain and his wicked sons that was troubling us, according to him; it was diabolical possession. We have to restore the unity of Christendom and exorcize these devils.

"He was a very pale, clean-shaven young man, with a fine clear-cut face, burning dark eyes and high-pitched tenor voice. He made few gestures and he kept his thin hands clenched as he talked. If he had been in the Roman Catholic Church instead of being just a High Anglican they would have set him to conduct missions. He had just that sort of eloquent intensity. And there he sat in his cassock, looking up and away over my shoulder and expounding the exorcism of the marshes.

"As he talked I could see that his head was full of long slow processions winding across the marshes with banners, canopies, vestments, boys chanting, censers swinging, priests asperging. I thought of the old vicar peering out of his dirty study window and I had a vision of him running out hoarse and stumbling, with murder in his eyes.

" 'But', I told him, 'there will be opposition!' and at that the manner of Mr Mortover changed. He stood up and threw out a stiff hand like an eagle's claw. 'It must be overcome!' said he, and in that instant I understood why men are killed in Belfast and Liverpool and Spain."

That was queer. I interrupted. "But, Dr Finchatton, what have Belfast and Liverpool and Spain to do with Cainsmarsh?" I asked.

That brought him to a stop for a moment. He looked at me with a very peculiar expression, something between suspicious scrutiny and obstinacy. "I was talking of Cainsmarsh," he said after deliberation.

"Then what have Belfast and Spain to do with it?"

"Nothing. I mentioned them, I suppose – by way of illustration... Let me get it! Let me get it! What I was thinking of was fanaticism. Both these men, the vicar and the priest, had their convictions – yes. High and noble convictions, no doubt, as they professed them. But what they really wanted to do was to fight. They wanted to be at each other's throats. That was where the haunting poison of the marsh came in. It wasn't their beliefs that stirred them, it was their fears. He wanted to shout and provoke...

"Well, – so for that matter did I. Why had I bawled and raved at the marsh out of my door overnight? And shaken my fist?"

He looked at me almost as if he expected me to answer.

"The Greeks had a word for it," he said; – "Panic. Endemic panic, that was the contagion of the marshes."

"That may be a name for it," I said. "But how much does that explain?"

"You realize," said Dr Finchatton, "that by this time I was in a headlong panic against panic. I felt that my time was running short. If I did not do something to exorcize it, the spirit of the Marsh would get me – surely. I should break. I should do something violent. I happened to have nothing very pressing just then to tie me, and I determined to play hookey from my consulting room for half a day and go over to Eastfolk museum. I would have a good reassuring look at those mammoth bones, which under the vicar's suggestion were beginning to take on far too human a form in my memory, and perhaps have a chat with the curator, who, I had heard, was an archaeologist of considerable ability.

"I found him a very pleasant little man, with a broad bland bare face and spectacles and a sort of watchfulness. He had that sort of watchfulness good photographers and portrait painters have, and it was the only thing that was not altogether comfortable about him. I caught him looking at me whenever I turned away from him...

"I professed a great interest in the flint implements which are so abundant in the low hills above the marshlands and about the series of human remains that had been unearthed there. He was an enthusiast and he found me intelligent. He embarked upon quite a history of the region. 'It must have been inhabited,' I said, 'for thousands of years.'

" 'Hundreds of thousands,' he told me. 'There were Neanderthalers and – But let me show you our special glory!'

"He led me to a locked glass cupboard in which was a thick lowering beetle-browed skull, that still seemed to scowl from its empty sockets. Beside it was its under-jaw. This dirty rusty brown treasure, he said, was the completest specimen of its kind in the world. It was almost unbroken. It had already settled a dozen controversies arising out of the fragmentary nature of its fellows. There were also a few vertebrae from the neck and a curved thigh-bone and a lot of smaller fragments in a case close

133

by, but the entire fissure in which these remains had been found had not yet been cleaned up, because the bones were half dissolved and very brittle and had to be extracted very carefully. The fissure was being worked with elaborate care. In the end they hoped to get almost an entire skeleton. Two or three very primitive and clumsy artefacts had also been found in this same cleft in the chalk, down which maybe the brute had slipped and been jammed and covered up. The little curator watched me as I surveyed his prize specimen and marked the snarling grin of its upper jaw and the shadowy vitality that still lurked in the caverns whence its eyes had once glared upon the world.

" 'That might, I suppose, be our ancestor?' I said.

" 'More probable than not.'

" '*That* in our blood!' I said.

"I turned half round and looked at the monster askance and when I spoke again I spoke as if he also might be listening. I asked a score of amateurish questions. There had been countless generations of him and his kind, I learnt. His sort had slouched and snarled over the marshes for a hundred times the length of all recorded history. In comparison with *his* overlordship our later human rule was a thing of yesterday. Millions of these brutish lives had come and passed, leaving fragments, implements, stones they had chipped or reddened by their fires, bones they had gnawed. Not a pebble in the marsh, not an inch of ground their feet had not pressed or their hands gripped a myriad times.

" 'Just something a little bit dreadful about him,' I said, talking vacuously while I made up my mind. Then I decided to put a question point-blank. I asked the curator had he heard – had he ever met the idea that the marsh was haunted?

"The scrutiny in the magnified eyes behind the glasses intensified. He had heard something.

" '*Well*,' said I.

"But he wanted me to speak first. He waited silently and so I was forced to go on. I told him practically all that I have told you. 'The marshes have got hold of me,' I said. 'And if I do not do something about it, they will drive me mad. I can't stand them and I have to stand them. Tell me why it is one dreams there so dismally, why one is haunted by fear in the daylight and horrible fears in the night?'

" 'You're not the first who has come to me with that question,' he said, still watching me.

" 'And you can tell me,' I said. 'What it is?'

" 'No,' he said.

"He was a careful man with his words as well as a watchful one with his eyes. He explained he went into the marsh to excavate and so he saw something of the people. 'They don't like these excavations,' he said. 'I have never heard of so much distrust of digging in any other part of the world. Maybe it is a strong local superstition. Maybe fear is contagious. They certainly fear. And I think they fear more today than they used to do. It is often very hard now to get permission to dig on private land.'

"I could see he was not telling me all he had in mind. He seemed to be saying things to me experimentally, as if he was trying out his ideas on me. He remarked that he never slept in the marsh even in the daytime. At times when he was sifting earth he would stop to listen, and resume sifting and then stop still again. 'Nothing to hear,' he said, 'and yet one gets strung up like that.'

135

"He came to a pause. I saw him looking very hard and with a peculiar expression at the cave-man's skull against the wall between us.

" 'You don't think an ugly beast like that could really leave a ghost?' I asked.

" 'It's left its bones,' he said. 'Do you think it had anything you could call a spirit? Something that might still be urgent to hurt and torment and frighten? Something profoundly suspicious and easily angered?'

"It was my turn to stare at him.

" 'You do not really believe that. You are suggesting that to me. For some purpose.'

"He laughed, still with a steady eye on me. 'If so, I have failed,' he said. 'But I did want to suggest it to you. If we can make a ghost of this fear of yours – well, ghosts can be laid. If we make a fever of it, fever can be cured. But while this remains merely panic fear and a smouldering rage, what can we do about it?'

" 'Very kind of you,' said I, 'to try and pull me together in that fashion, truss my mind, so to speak, for exorcism. It isn't so easy as that.'

"And then," said Dr Finchatton, "he switched off that hypnotic bespectacled stare of his and began to talk to me more frankly.

"What he said was rather metaphysical," Dr Finchatton said, "and I am not much of a metaphysician. It was queer theoretical stuff and yet, in a way, it had a sort of air of explanation. I will try and tell it you as well as I can. The expression he used was that we were breaking the frame of our present – the Frame of our Present?"

Dr Finchatton looked at me enquiringly. I remained judicial. I had not the remotest idea what the frame of our present might be. "Go on," I said.

"He stood with his profile to me, no longer watching me, looking out of the window and saying what was in his mind. 'A century or so ago,' he said, 'men lived in the present far more than they do now. Their past went back four or five thousand years, their future hardly went as far; they lived for *now*. And what they called the eternities. They knew nothing of the remote real past. They cared nothing for the real future. *That*' – and he nodded at the cave-man's skull – 'just wasn't there. All that was buried and forgotten and out of life. We lived in a magic sphere and we felt taken care of and safe. And now in the last century or so, we have broken that. We have poked into the past, unearthing age after age and we peer more and more forward into the future. And that's what's the matter with us.'

" 'In the marsh?' said I.

" 'Everywhere. Your vicar and priest know that by instinct though they don't know how to express it – or anyhow they don't express it as you and I do. Sometimes it's nearer the surface in the marsh – but it's everywhere. We have broken the frame of the present, and the past, the long black past of fear and hate that our grandfathers never knew of, never suspected, is pouring back upon us. And the future opens like a gulf to swallow us up. The animal fears again and the animal rages again and the old faiths no longer restrain it. The cave-man, the ancestral ape, the ancestral brute have returned. So it is. I can assure you I am talking realities to you. It is going on now everywhere. You have been in the marsh. You have felt them in the marsh, but I tell you these resurrected savageries are breathing now and thrusting

137

everywhere. The world is full of menace – not only here.' He stopped short and his spectacles flashed as he looked at me and then stared again out of the window.

" 'But,' said I, 'this is all very fine and mystical but how does it help me? What am I to do?'

"He said this was a mental thing and it had to be fought out in the mind.

" 'I have to go back to the marsh this evening.'

"He went on saying that the frame of the present was shattered and could never be restored. I had to open out – 'open out', he said – and enlarge my mind to a vaster world where the cave-man was as present as the daily paper and a thousand years ahead was on the doorstep. 'That is all very well,' I said, 'but what does it mean? What am *I* to do now? I am asking you; what am *I* to do now?'

"His regard came back to me. 'Fight it out if you can,' he said. 'Go back. You won't escape by running away. Go back and have one more round with whatever you choose to fancy it, the Evil, the Fear, the Ghost of Cain or *that* fellow's ghost – '

"He paused and we both looked round at the clumsy skull as though we felt it might have something to say in the matter.

" 'Broaden your mind to the new scale,' he resumed, rather more confidentially. 'Face it if you can. And then if you still find you are slipping, you must try to get help. You should go off to London and have a definite treatment. The man you should see is Norbert, of – I think it is 391 Harley Street, but I can get that for you. He has been one of the first men to realize this spreading miasma of the mind of which you are suffering and devise some sort of treatment for it. To tell you the truth, he has helped me. Though his methods are rough and strange. I had some slight touch of your trouble, and as I happened to know about him I called him in. And early. He flies over to Les Noupets once or twice a week. There's a clinic over there...'

"So much for the curator of the Eastfolk museum. For the time he pulled me together. His modern scientific lingo was something I could understand. I felt that I was no longer being hunted darkly and strangely and beyond any possibility of help; I was just an experimentalist facing a disagreeable and risky but by no means impossible challenge.

"But I had no luck in that last round with the ghosts of the cave-men," said Dr Finchatton. "I went back while it was still daylight. At the very outset before I reached my house I came upon something dreadful. It was a dog that had been beaten to death. Yes; beaten to death! You may think that in this world where so many terrible things are happening a cruelly ill-treated dog was no great matter. It was to me.

"I saw it lying among the nettles by the roadside. I thought some motorist must have run over it and thrown it aside. I got down to look at it and make sure that it was dead. It wasn't simply dead; it was battered to a pulp. With some blunt heavy instrument. There couldn't have been a whole bone left in it. Somebody must have rained blows upon it, a frantic whirlwind of blows.

"For a medical man I know I am over-sensitive. At any rate I went on through the sunshine in a state of horror, at nature, at the deep fountains of cruelty in the human make-up. What frantic outburst had destroyed that poor brute? And then I had hardly been back in my house ten minutes when another shock arrived. This again may seem a small matter to you. To me it was overwhelming. A breathless messenger came on a bicycle from

139

the vicarage of Cross in Slackness. He was so scared that for some moments I could not understand what he was telling me, and then I realized that old Rawdon had set upon his poor old wife and done his best to kill her. He had knocked her down and beaten her. 'The poor old lady!' gasped the boy. 'You better come soon. We got him tied up in the outhouse and she's on the bed upstairs scared to death – too frightened to speak. He's raving something frightful. Frightful. Says she tried to poison him… The language!…'

"I brought out my car again and went over. I managed what I could to make the poor old thing comfortable; he hadn't hurt her so much as I feared, a few bruises but no bones broken, and it was chiefly shock and amazement she suffered from; and presently two policemen came and carried off old Rawdon to the police station at Holdingham. I wouldn't go down to see him. She spoke just a word or two as she lay there. 'Edward!' she muttered and then in amazement 'Oh *Edward!*' And then sharply with a note of terror *'Edward!'* and a weak scream. I gave her a sleeping-draught and arranged for a woman to stay the night with her and then I went back to my own place.

"So long as I was actively employed I kept going, but as soon as I got home I found myself slumping. I could eat nothing. I drank a lot of whisky and instead of going to bed I fell asleep in an arm-chair by the fire. I awoke in terror and found the fire nearly out. I went to bed and when at last I got to sleep the dreams closed in on me and I sat up again starkly awake. I got up and put on an old dressing-gown and went downstairs and made up the fire, determined to keep awake at any cost. But I dozed there and then went back to bed. And so between the bed and the fireside I dragged through the night. My dreams were all a mix-up of the poor scared old lady, the almost as pitiful old man, the ideas the museum custodian had put in my head and, brooding over it all, that infernal palaeolithic skull.

"More and more did the threat of that primordial Adamite dominate me. I could not banish that eyeless stare and that triumphant grin from my mind, sleeping or waking. Waking I saw it as it was in the museum, as if it was a living presence that had set us a riddle and was amused to hear our inadequate attempts at a solution. Sleeping I saw it released from all rational proportions. It became gigantic. It became as vast as a cliff, a mountainous skull in which the orbits and hollows of the jaw were huge caves. He had an effect – it is hard to convey these dream effects – as if he was continually rising and yet he was always towering there. In the foreground I saw his innumerable descendants, swarming like ants, swarms of human beings hurrying to and fro, making helpless gestures of submission or deference, resisting an overpowering impulse to throw themselves under his all-devouring shadow. Presently these swarms began to fall into lines and columns, were clad in uniforms, formed up and began marching and trotting towards the black shadows under those worn and rust-stained teeth. From which darkness there presently oozed something – something winding and trickling, and something that manifestly tasted very agreeably to him. Blood."

And then Finchatton said a queer thing. "Little children killed by air-raids in the street."

I made no comment. I remained quietly attentive. It was an "aside", as actors used to say. He took up his story where he had left it.

"Morning," he resumed after an introspective pause, "found me frantic at the telephone. At great pains and what I am afraid will prove ruinous expense to me, I managed to secure a locum-tenens and forthwith I bolted off to London, gripping my sanity so to speak with both hands, to see this man Norbert. And it is Norbert who has sent me here... Norbert you know is a very extraordinary man. He was not at all what I had expected."

Dr Finchatton stopped short. He looked at me. "That's all."

I nodded silently.

"Well," he said, "what do you make of it?"

"In a day or so, perhaps, I shall begin to think something about it. At present I don't know what to say. It's incredible and yet – you almost make me believe it. I mean I don't think it really happened – I wouldn't go so far as that – but I believe it happened to you."

"Exactly. I'm glad to be able to talk to a man like you. It's what Norbert wants me to do. He wants me to familiarize myself with what has just happened to me, just in the spirit in which you have taken it, so as to be able to distinguish between the realities of my experience, the realities of life, he calls them, and the fears and fancies and dreams I have wrapped about them. His idea is that I ought to see things *unfeelingly*. Because after all – what do you think?" He looked at me very earnestly.

"How much of what I have been telling you is actual concrete happening and how much – what shall I call it? – mental reaction? Old Rawdon attacking his wife – that was real. That broken-up dog was real... Norbert's idea, you know, is that I should talk it quietly over with anyone who – who seems reasonably balanced and not too worried about the past or the future. So as to get these facts as facts and not as dreads and horrors. He wants to bring me back so to speak to what he calls a rational insensitiveness, rational insensitiveness, that's his formula, and so get a firmer foothold for – whatever I have to do next."

He gulped down his wine. "It's very good of you to have listened to me," he said, and then as a shadow fell across the terrace before us: "*Hullo!*"

# CHAPTER FOUR

## The Intolerable Psychiatrist

I disliked the shadow of Dr Norbert even before I looked up and saw him. He was and he meant to be an overwhelming sort of man, and though I am indolent, self-indulgent and unenterprising I can be as obstinate as a whole team of mules. I braced myself for opposition to whatever he wanted or had to say before he opened his mouth.

He was not at all the sort of person I should have expected a psychotherapeutist to be. A psychotherapeutist I think ought to have calm eyes and a reassuring manner – and a certain general neatness of self-control. He ought to look fresh and healthy and this fellow was distinctly cadaverous. He was large and expansive and untidy with lots of undisciplined black hair and thick eyebrows, and his large dark and flashing eyes either rolled about in his more voluble moments or came to a focus in a dramatic pause and glared at you – not a steady look but a glare that pushed at your face and was supported by an immense frown. His features were uniformly large, and he had the loose mouth of an orator and a voice of remarkable amplitude. He wore an old-fashioned upstanding white collar and a loose black bow tie very much under one ear. It was as if he had dressed himself once for all in some remote pre-war fashion and never changed it since. He looked much more like an actor on vacation than a psychotherapeutist. He made me think of the old *Punch* pictures of the Grand Old Man, or Henry Irving or Thomas Carlyle. A more unsuitable figure to interrupt a couple of decent-looking modern Englishmen sitting over their apéritifs on the terrace of the Perona Source Hotel it would be hard to imagine.

But there he was, entirely unlike anything I could have foreseen, the great Dr Norbert, Finchatton's mental healer, hands on hips, looking down on me in his most impressive manner. Finchatton had described him as unexpected, but the last thing I should have expected was anything so large, so oracular and so antique.

"I have been watching you from above," he said as though he was God Almighty. "I didn't want to interrupt while Finchatton was telling his tale. But now I perceive you have got through with it and I pounce."

Finchatton looked at me with a sort of silent entreaty to bear with Norbert's extraordinary manner and hear him out.

"You've heard his story?" Norbert demanded of me.

His manner did nothing to veil the fact that he was the psychotherapeutist and Finchatton was his "case". "He told you about how the cave-man dawned upon his mind? He talked about that terror in Cainsmarsh. Good! And the growing realization of evil? Well, – how have you reacted to that? What do you, with your manifestly very normal mind, make of it?"

He thrust his great face, all interrogation, some inches towards me. "Tell me in your own words," he said, and waited like a teacher examining a child.

"Dr Finchatton," said I, "has been relating some very extraordinary things. Yes. But I should have to think them over a lot before I could pass judgment upon them."

Norbert made the grimace of a teacher dealing with a stupid child.

"But *I* want your reactions now. Before you think."

"You *may* want," said I to myself. "I can't," I said aloud.

"But it will be of very great importance to Dr Finchatton for you to tell me now. Never mind why."

Suddenly I heard a clock striking. "Good heavens!" I cried, standing up and throwing a ten-franc note to the hovering waiter. "I shall keep my aunt waiting for lunch! That will *never* do."

"But you *can't* leave this business like this!" said Norbert, featuring an incredulous amazement. "You can't. It's your duty to a fellow-creature in trouble to hear this case out and help to rationalize it. You *must* help us." Glare. "Positively I *can't* release you."

I turned to Finchatton. "If Dr Finchatton," I said, "would like to talk about it some more…"

"Of course he wants to talk to you some more."

I kept my eyes on Finchatton, who nodded with an intensified appeal.

"I'll come again," I said. "Tomorrow. About this time. But I can't stay now… It's impossible."

I went down the winding road at something between a walk and a trot – really concerned to be so late, because you know my aunt is simply awful if anyone keeps her waiting for lunch. I was already doubtful about the promise I had given and a little angry at having been forced to make it. It was as if I had

147

admitted some preposterous claim upon my attention and had bought myself off.

I turned my head and saw the two men among those above me, side by side, Norbert overshadowing Finchatton.

"Tomorrow," I called – though I suppose I was well out of earshot.

Norbert made a large gesture.

Now I did not want in the least to see this Dr Norbert any more. I had indeed conceived a violent antipathy for him. I did not like his "You-and-Finchatton-are-rabbits-and-now-I-am-going-to-dissect-you" style. I did not like his large enveloping voice nor the way his brow and purpose seemed to overhang the rest of him. And I detest angular commanding gestures made with arms that are much too long. But on the other hand I had taken a real liking to Dr Finchatton and developed a very lively interest in his story. I thought he had told it very vividly. I wish I could convey the conviction of his manner in this transcript. Directly I got away from him I began to think of questions I might have asked him and to want to see him again. I regarded Norbert as a nuisance who had just butted in upon an interesting tale. I dismissed Norbert from my mind and went on thinking of Finchatton.

There was something about this story of a magic marshland into which a man might go sane and confident, admiring the butterflies and the flowers, and out of which presently he would come running again frantic with fear and rage, that had seized hold upon my imagination very strongly. And the way in which that evil old skull, that ancestral skull, lurking unseen at first in the background, had slowly become visible – ! It was like something being lit up behind a transparency. It was an explanation that was itself an enigma. And now, degree by degree, those bare jaws were being clad and covered until a phantom lip framed the grinning teeth, and there were dark aggressive bloodshot eyes below the beetling brows. The cave-man was becoming more and more plainly a living presence as the story germinated in my mind.

It was a face at last and not a skull that watched me out of that dream story. It was absurd, but indeed it seemed to be watching me. It watched me all that evening and it mopped and mowed in the night. It made me inattentive so that in the afternoon my combinations at croquet were unusually shortsighted and poor, and in the evening I offended my aunt deeply by failing to play up to my usual form. She was against me, but as she reckoned on my playing up to my usual form, she was surprised and perplexed by the things I did and put quite off her game, so that she and her partner lost heavily. But I scarcely heeded her reproaches and I undressed slowly, my mind full of that distant marshland so mysteriously accursed, so monstrously overshadowed now by that brutish revenant. I sat for quite a long time thinking it over before I went to bed.

Next day I got up to the Perona Source Hotel rather late. I had meant to be early. I would have taken a tram but an *agent* explained they were not running. There had been a lightning strike organized by the Communists and there had been a fight at the depot in which several people had been injured. 'One must be firm these days,' said the agent. Consequently I had to walk the whole way. And it was bad luck I thought, to find Dr Norbert stretching out his long legs under a table umbrella on the terrace and no signs of Dr Finchatton. Norbert motioned for me to join him and I sat down on a green chair beside his table. I did so reluctantly. I wanted to make it plain that it was Finchatton I wanted to see. I wanted more of the story and I did not want any mental probing, judgment dissection, earnest invasion of my private thoughts by this pretentious individual.

"Where's your friend?" I asked.

"He cannot come down today. It is just as well."

"I thought he had arranged – "

"*He* thought he had arranged –  But he was prevented. As I say, it is just as well."

"I don't see that."

"From *my* point of view. I want very much to get a common-sense outside view of this story that fills his mind. I want it for my own sake as well as his."

"But how can you expect me to contribute?"

"Well – for one simple thing; do you know any part of the world called Cainsmarsh?"

He turned round to look at me as he might have looked at an animal he had just given an injection.

"I imagined it was somewhere in fenland."

"There is no such district in the world."

"It is a pseudonym?"

"It is a myth."

He surveyed me for a moment and then decided that for the present I was not worth watching. He put his two long hands palm to palm in front of him and spoke with great deliberation staring out to sea. "Our friend," he said, "*was* a doctor near Ely. Everything he told you was true and everything he told you was a lie. He is troubled beyond reason by certain things and the only way in which he can express them even to himself is by a fable."

"But some of these things – really happened?"

"Oh yes. There *was* a case of gross cruelty to a dog. There *was* a poor old drunken parson who beat his wife. Things of that sort are happening all over the world every day. They are in the nature of things. If you cannot accept things like that, sir, *you cannot live*. And Finchatton really went to the Tressider Museum at Ely, and Cunningham, the custodian, had the sense to spot his condition and send him on to me. But the mischief was already done to him before he went into the marsh. He's told you practically everything – but as though he showed it through bottle glass that distorted it all. And the reason why he has made it all up into that story – "

Dr Norbert turned upon me, putting his arms akimbo and glaring at my face. He spoke with slow deliberation, as if he was speaking in capital letters, " – is because the realities that are overwhelming him are so monstrous and frightful that he has to transform them into this fairy tale about old skulls and silences in butterfly land, in the hope of getting them down to the dimensions of an hallucination and so presently expelling them from his thoughts."

The expression of his face made me uncomfortable. I turned and beckoned the waiter for another vermouth in order to recover my composure. "And what," I asked offhandedly, "may those more terrible realities be?"

"Do you never read a daily newspaper?" asked Dr Norbert.

"Not very intently. Most of the stuff seems to me to be either pompous or wilfully disagreeable. But I do *The Times* Cross-Word Puzzle nearly every day. And I read most of the tennis and croquet stuff and so on. Have I missed much?"

"You've missed the things that have made Finchatton mad."

"Mad?"

"Didn't he repeat my phrase? – endemic panic? A contagion in our atmosphere. A sickness in the very grounds of our lives, breaking out here and there and filling men's minds with a paralysing, irrational fear?"

"He did use that expression."

"Yes, sir. And it is what I am dealing with here. It is what even I am only beginning to realize. A new Plague – of the soul. A distress of the mind that has long lurked in odd corners of the mind, an endemic disorder, rising suddenly and spreading into a world epidemic. The story our friend put away into a sort of fairyland fenland is really the story of thousands of people today –and it will be the story of hundreds of thousands tomorrow. You are untroubled. As yet... Maybe you are immune... It is most important to me just now in my study of this increasing malaise that I should realize the reaction of an uninfected mind."

"I've never been good soil for out-of-the-way ideas," I said. "Still I don't want to take any risks. You don't think that presently I too shall begin to be frightened of the dark and scared in the open, and see ancestral apes and savages looming up over the world?"

He put his big hand across the table and pressed my arm for a moment. "If you do," he said, glaring portentously, "have courage."

It flashed into my mind abruptly that this man was really as mad or madder than Finchatton. I put the question to him pat.

"Dr Norbert, have *you* by any chance – got infected?"

The glare became intensified. He lifted up his face so to speak and then brought it down like a hammer on the word.

"Yes."

He spoke with such emphasis that my face was bedewed.

"I was an early case," he said. "I had to deal with myself. There was nobody to help me. I had to study myself. I have been through it all, sir. And crawled out on the other side. A salted man, immunized. At the price of a monstrous struggle…"

And with that he launched out upon the most astonishing dissertation I have ever heard. He made a little pause before the discourse came. What he had to say couldn't be said very well from a lounge chair. Presently he was sitting up and gripping his chair with both hands. Then he stood up and talked and walked about the terrace in front of me – no longer talking so much as orating. I have a fairly retentive memory but it would be impossible for me now to give you a full report of all the strange tissue of assertion and arguments he poured forth. Some of his phrases and terms of thought I will quote. Finchatton's story had sounded like fantasy. This had no quality of fantasy about it at all. It began like pseudo-science and philosophy, but gradually it became more and more a booming, disconcerting exhortation. We were to take hold of life – *grip* it. Some of his ideas Finchatton had already handed on to me. I recognized the phrases. There was that about 'breaking the Frame of the Present'.

"But what does that *mean?*" I said almost irritably.

"Animals," he said, "live wholly in the present. They are framed in immediate things. So are really unsophisticated people. Israeli, Sands, Murphy, a crowd of people have been working on that." He rattled off a score of names but these are all that I remember. "But we men, we have been probing and piercing into the past and future. We have been multiplying memories, histories, traditions, we have filled ourselves with forebodings and plannings and apprehensions. And so our worlds have become overwhelmingly vast for us, terrific, appalling.

Things that had seemed forgotten for ever have suddenly come back into the very present of our consciousness."

"In other words," said I, trying to keep him moored to current realities, "we have found out about the cave-man."

"Found out about him!" he shouted. "We live in his presence. He has never died. He is anything but dead. Only – "

He came close and tapped my shoulder. " – Only he was shut off from us and hidden. For a long time. And now we see him here face to face and his grin derides us. Man is still what he was. Invincibly bestial, envious, malicious, greedy. Man, sir, unmasked and disillusioned is the same fearing, snarling, fighting beast he was a hundred thousand years ago. These are no metaphors, sir. What I tell you is the monstrous reality. The brute has been marking time and dreaming of a progress it has failed to make. Any archaeologist will tell you as much; modern man has no better skull, no better brain. Just a cave-man, more or less trained. There has been no real change, no real escape. Civilization, progress, all *that*, we are discovering, was a delusion. Nothing was secured. Nothing. For a time man built himself in, into his neat little *present* world of Gods and Providences, rainbow promises and so forth. It was artificial, it was artistic, fictitious. We are only beginning to realize *how* artificial. Now it is breaking down, Mr Frobisher. It is breaking down all about us and we seem unable to prevent it. We *seem*... No escape appears. No, sir. Civilization so far has been a feeble, inadaptable falsity. And now it is found out; Fate has been too much for it. A stunning realization, sir! And when sensitive, unprepared men like our poor friend Finchatton become aware of it, they show themselves too weak to face it. They refuse to face a world so grim and great as this world really is. They take refuge in stories of hauntings and personal madness – in the hope of some sort of exorcism, something they think will be a cure… There is no such cure. There is no such way now of dressing up these facts and putting them aside.

"So, sir, they have to be faced," he roared. "They have to be faced." He seemed to be addressing himself not simply to me but to some large public meeting. His vast gestures ignored me. "The time when men could be put in blinkers to save them from seeing too much is past. Past for ever! There can be no more religions of reassurance. No churches of 'There – there!' *That* sort of thing is at an end."

"And then?" said I very quietly. Because the louder he shouted, the more coldly resistant I became.

He sat down and gripped my arm again. He became persuasively confidential. From bawling, his voice sank to a deep heavy undertone. "Madness, sir, from the mental side, is poor Nature's answer to overwhelming fact. It is flight. And today all over the world, *intellectual men are going mad!* They are dithering, because they realize that the fight against this cave-man who is over us, who is in us, who is indeed *us*, is going against these imaginary selves. The world is no longer safe for anything. It was sheer delusion that we had Him under. Him! The pursuing brute who never desists."

By a movement that I hoped seemed inadvertent, I freed my arm from his clutch. I had an absurd feeling that I was like that wedding guest who was gripped by the Ancient Mariner. "But then," I said, putting my hands in my pockets and leaning back so as to be out of reach of any fresh attempt to grab me; "What do you think you are doing with Finchatton? What do you think has to be done?"

Dr Norbert waved his arms about and then stood up. "I tell you, sir," he said, shouting down at me as though I was a score of yards off, "in the end he has to do what we all have to do. Face the facts! Face the facts, sir! Go through with it. Survive if you can and perish if you can't. Do as I have done and shape your mind to a new scale. Only giants can save the world from complete relapse and so we – we who care for civilization – have to become giants. We have to bind a harder, stronger civilization like steel about the world. We have to make such a mental effort as the stars have never witnessed yet. Arise, O mind of Man!" (He called me that!) "Or be for ever defeated."

I wanted to say I preferred to be defeated without making any fuss about it, but he gave me no chance to say that.

For now indeed he was fairly raving. There was even a touch of froth on his lips. He paced up and down and talked on and on, in a fine frenzy.

I suppose from first to last throughout the ages decent people of my sort have had to listen to this kind of thing, but it seemed to me beyond all reason that I should have to listen to it on the terrace of the Source Hotel at Perona above Les Noupets on a lovely morning in this year of grace nineteen hundred and thirty-six. He was striding up and down now like a Hebrew prophet. It may look all right as a part of history, this sort of rhetoric, this epoch-making and all that, but in real life it is hoarse and outrageous. It's damned bad manners – to be plain about it. I ceased to mark or remember half the things he said.

There was no answering it. One could as soon swim up the falls of Niagara.

He made it more and more plain that he was exhorting me. Me personally. I never had such a ballyragging. He was warning me to brace my mind to escape from the Wrath to Come. He called it that – 'Wrath to Come'. He made me think of Peter the Hermit raging through the quiet cities of eleventh-century Christendom and starting all that trouble about the Crusades. He made me think of Savonarola and John Knox and all the disturbing people who have rushed shouting across history – leaving it very much as they found it, telling people to give up their lives, go to their tents, O Israel, take up arms, storm the Tuileries, smash the Winter Palace, and a score of such outrageous things. At little old Les Noupets, mind you.

He reeled off a list of atrocities, murders and horrors all over the world. I suppose there *is* a rather unusual amount of massacre and torture going on nowadays. I suppose the outlook *is* pretty black. I suppose there may be frightful wars, air raids and pogroms ahead of us. But what am *I* to do about it? What was the good of bow-wow-wowing at me? The intensity of his manner could not hide the fact that he had no certitude even in his own mind, that at best he was struggling with only the blank shadows of ideas. Whenever I tried to get in an enquiring word, he would raise his voice and boom over me. "I tell you!" he would roar up.

But that was just what he didn't do – and apparently couldn't do.

"In a little while," he said, "there will be no ease, no security, no comfort any more." (Thank Heaven! he did not say I was 'living on the brink of a volcano'.) "There will be no choice before a human being but to be either a driven animal or a stern devotee to that true civilization, that disciplined civilization, that has never yet been achieved. Victim or Vigilante. And that, my

157

friend, means you! I say it to *you! You!*" And he pointed a lean forefinger.

As there was no one else present – for the waiter had gone inside – there was no reason whatever for that 'you' and that pointing finger. Just want of proportion…

Yet – It is a most unpleasant thing to admit but these two men *have* in a sort of way hypnotized me after all, and put something of this anxiety and something of this haunting of theirs upon me. I try and get them in a proper perspective by writing down this story, but the mere writing of it makes me realize how much I can't detach myself. I can no more get rid of it by telling it to you than Finchatton could get rid of it by telling it to me. I did not know that one could be hypnotized in this fashion, by people just sitting about or talking to you. I thought you had to sit still and give yourself up to hypnotism or else there was nothing doing. But now I find I don't sleep as well as I used to do, I catch myself anxious about world affairs, I read evil things between the lines in the newspapers, and usually very faintly but sometimes quite plainly I see, behind the transparent front of things, that cave-man face… How was it Finchatton put it? – "continually rising and yet always towering up there". And I have to admit I am not so even-tempered as I was in conversation. The other day I even contradicted my aunt with some asperity, to our mutual astonishment. And I snapped at a waiter…

I did not realize the seriousness of this business until I had this scene with Norbert. That was what made me so restive and after I broke away from him I took care to see no more of him or Finchatton. Yet all the same the mischief had been started in me and it grows. In those two brief mornings, I got myself infected, fool that I was to listen to them! And now the infection is working in me.

I resent the whole business. What is the good of putting this horror of Cainsmarsh upon a man and not telling him exactly what to do about it? I *do* realize that our present world is going to pieces. I quite see that we are still under the sway of the caveman and that he is staging a tremendous come-back. I am surprised I didn't see all that before. Already I have dreams about that giant skull, quite unpleasant dreams. But what is the good of talking about them? If I told my aunt any of this, she would say I was off my head. What can a fellow like me do about it all?

Study it up – enlarge my mind to a new scale? Become "giant-minded"? *What* a phrase! Build up a new civilization of steel and power in the place of the one that is collapsing?... Me?... Look at my bringing up? Is it *in* me?

It is too much to expect of our sort of people.

I'm ready to fall in with anything that seems promising. I'm all for peace, order, social justice, service and all that. But if I'm to *think!* If I'm to find out what to do with myself!

That's too much.

I made my break-away from Norbert's flooding eloquence that morning with some considerable difficulty. I stood up. "I must be going," I said. "I have to play croquet with my aunt at half past twelve."

"But what does croquet matter," he cried in that intolerable voice of his, "if your world is falling in ruins about you?"

He made a move almost as though he would impede my retreat. He just wanted to go on being apocalyptic. But I had had enough of this apocalyptic stuff.

I looked him in the face, firmly but politely. I said, "I don't care. The world *may* be going to pieces. The Stone Age may be returning. This may, as you say, be the sunset of civilization. I'm sorry, but I can't help it this morning. I have other engagements. All the same – laws of the Medes and Persians – I am going to play croquet with my aunt at half past twelve today."

# H G WELLS

## THE HISTORY OF MR POLLY

Mr Polly is one of literature's most enduring and universal creations. An ordinary man, trapped in an ordinary life, Mr Polly makes a series of ill-advised choices that bring him to the very brink of financial ruin. Determined not to become the latest victim of the economic retrenchment of the Edwardian age, he rebels in magnificent style and takes control of his life once and for all.

ISBN 0-7551-0404-8

# H G Wells

## In the Days of the Comet

Revenge was all Leadford could think of as he set out to find the unfaithful Nettie and her adulterous lover. But this was all to change when a new comet entered the earth's orbit and totally reversed the natural order of things. The Great Change had occurred and any previous emotions, thoughts, ambitions, hopes and fears had all been removed. Free love, pacifism and equality were now the name of the game. But how would Leadford fare in this most utopian of societies?

ISBN 0-7551-0406-4

# H G WELLS

## THE INVISIBLE MAN

On a cold wintry day in the depths of February a stranger
appeared in The Coach and Horses requesting a room. So
strange was this man's appearance, dressed from head to foot
with layer upon layer of clothing, bandages and the most
enormous glasses, that the owner, Mrs Hall, quite wondered
what accident could have befallen him. She didn't know then that
he was invisible – but the rumours soon began to spread…

H G Wells' masterpiece *The Invisible Man* is a classic science-
fiction thriller showing the perils of scientific advancement.

ISBN 0-7551-0407-2

# H G WELLS

## THE ISLAND OF DR MOREAU

A shipwreck in the South Seas brings a doctor to an island paradise. Far from seeing this as the end of his life, Dr Moreau seizes the opportunity to play God and infiltrate a reign of terror in this new kingdom. Endless cruel and perverse experiments ensue and see a series of new creations – the 'Beast People' – all of which must bow before the deified doctor.

Originally a Swiftian satire on the dangers of authority and submission, Wells' *The Island of Dr Moreau* can now just as well be read as a prophetic tale of genetic modification and mutability.

ISBN 0-7551-0408-0

# H G WELLS

## MEN LIKE GODS

Mr Barnstaple was ever such a careful driver, careful to indicate before every manoeuvre and very much in favour of slowing down at the slightest hint of difficulty. So however could he have got the car into a skid on a bend on the Maidenhead road?

When he recovered himself he was more than a little relieved to see the two cars that he had been following still merrily motoring along in front of him. It seemed that all was well – except that the scenery had changed, rather a lot. It was then that the awful truth dawned: Mr Barnstaple had been hurled into another world altogether.

How would he ever survive in this supposed Utopia, and more importantly, how would he ever get back?

ISBN 0-7551-0413-7

# H G WELLS

## THE WAR OF THE WORLDS

'No one would have believed in the last years of the nineteenth century that this world was being watched keenly and closely by intelligences greater than man's...'

A series of strange atmospheric disturbances on the planet Mars may raise concern on Earth but it does little to prepare the inhabitants for imminent invasion. At first the odd-looking Martians seem to pose no threat for the intellectual powers of Victorian London, but it seems man's superior confidence is disastrously misplaced. For the Martians are heading towards victory with terrifying velocity.

*The War of the Worlds* is an expertly crafted invasion story that can be read as a frenzied satire on the dangers of imperialism and occupation.

ISBN 0-7551-0426-9

## OTHER TITLES BY H G WELLS AVAILABLE DIRECT
## FROM HOUSE OF STRATUS

| Quantity | £ | $(US) | $(CAN) | € |
|---|---|---|---|---|
| **FICTION** | | | | |
| ANN VERONICA | 9.99 | 14.95 | 22.95 | 16.50 |
| APROPOS OF DOLORES | 9.99 | 14.95 | 22.95 | 16.50 |
| THE AUTOCRACY OF MR PARHAM | 9.99 | 14.95 | 22.95 | 16.50 |
| BABES IN THE DARKLING WOOD | 9.99 | 14.95 | 22.95 | 16.50 |
| BEALBY | 9.99 | 14.95 | 22.95 | 16.50 |
| BRYNHILD | 9.99 | 14.95 | 22.95 | 16.50 |
| THE BULPINGTON OF BLUP | 9.99 | 14.95 | 22.95 | 16.50 |
| THE DREAM | 9.99 | 14.95 | 22.95 | 16.50 |
| THE FIRST MEN IN THE MOON | 9.99 | 14.95 | 22.95 | 16.50 |
| THE FOOD OF THE GODS | 9.99 | 14.95 | 22.95 | 16.50 |
| THE HISTORY OF MR POLLY | 9.99 | 14.95 | 22.95 | 16.50 |
| THE HOLY TERROR | 9.99 | 14.95 | 22.95 | 16.50 |
| IN THE DAYS OF THE COMET | 9.99 | 14.95 | 22.95 | 16.50 |
| THE INVISIBLE MAN | 7.99 | 12.95 | 19.95 | 14.50 |
| THE ISLAND OF DR MOREAU | 7.99 | 12.95 | 19.95 | 14.50 |
| KIPPS: THE STORY OF A SIMPLE SOUL | 9.99 | 14.95 | 22.95 | 16.50 |
| LOVE AND MR LEWISHAM | 9.99 | 14.95 | 22.95 | 16.50 |
| MARRIAGE | 9.99 | 14.95 | 22.95 | 16.50 |
| MEANWHILE | 9.99 | 14.95 | 22.95 | 16.50 |
| MEN LIKE GODS | 9.99 | 14.95 | 22.95 | 16.50 |
| A MODERN UTOPIA | 9.99 | 14.95 | 22.95 | 16.50 |
| MR BRITLING SEES IT THROUGH | 9.99 | 14.95 | 22.95 | 16.50 |

ALL HOUSE OF STRATUS BOOKS ARE AVAILABLE FROM GOOD BOOKSHOPS
OR DIRECT FROM THE PUBLISHER:

**Internet:** **www.houseofstratus.com** including synopses and features.

**Email:** **sales@houseofstratus.com**
**info@houseofstratus.com**
(please quote author, title and credit card details.)

## OTHER TITLES BY H G WELLS AVAILABLE DIRECT
## FROM HOUSE OF STRATUS

| Quantity | | £ | $(US) | $(CAN) | € |
|---|---|---|---|---|---|
| **FICTION** | | | | | |
| | THE NEW MACHIAVELLI | 9.99 | 14.95 | 22.95 | 16.50 |
| | THE PASSIONATE FRIENDS | 9.99 | 14.95 | 22.95 | 16.50 |
| | THE SEA LADY | 7.99 | 12.95 | 19.95 | 14.50 |
| | THE SHAPE OF THINGS TO COME | 9.99 | 14.95 | 22.95 | 16.50 |
| | THE TIME MACHINE | 7.99 | 12.95 | 19.95 | 14.50 |
| | TONO-BUNGAY | 9.99 | 14.95 | 22.95 | 16.50 |
| | THE UNDYING FIRE | 7.99 | 12.95 | 19.95 | 14.50 |
| | THE WAR IN THE AIR | 9.99 | 14.95 | 22.95 | 16.50 |
| | THE WAR OF THE WORLDS | 7.99 | 12.95 | 19.95 | 14.50 |
| | THE WHEELS OF CHANCE | 7.99 | 12.95 | 19.95 | 14.50 |
| | WHEN THE SLEEPER WAKES | 9.99 | 14.95 | 22.95 | 16.50 |
| | THE WIFE OF SIR ISAAC HARMAN | 9.99 | 14.95 | 22.95 | 16.50 |
| | THE WONDERFUL VISIT | 7.99 | 12.95 | 19.95 | 14.50 |
| | THE WORLD OF WILLIAM CLISSOLD | | | | |
| | VOLUMES 1,2,3 | 12.99 | 19.95 | 29.95 | 22.00 |
| **NON-FICTION** | | | | | |
| | THE CONQUEST OF TIME *AND* | | | | |
| | THE HAPPY TURNING | 7.99 | 12.95 | 19.95 | 14.50 |
| | EXPERIMENT IN AUTOBIOGRAPHY | | | | |
| | VOLUMES 1,2 | 12.99 | 19.95 | 29.95 | 22.00 |
| | H G WELLS IN LOVE | 9.99 | 14.95 | 22.95 | 16.50 |
| | THE OPEN CONSPIRACY AND | | | | |
| | OTHER WRITINGS | 9.99 | 14.95 | 22.95 | 16.50 |

| | | |
|---|---|---|
| **Tel:** | Order Line | **International** |
| | 0800 169 1780 (UK) | +44 (0) 1845 527700 (UK) |
| | 1 800 724 1100 (USA) | +01    845 463 1100 (USA) |
| **Fax:** | +44 (0) 1845 527711 (UK) | |
| | +01    845 463 0018 (USA) | |
| | (please quote author, title and credit card details.) | |
| **Send to:** | House of Stratus Sales Department | House of Stratus Inc. |
| | Thirsk Industrial Park | 2 Neptune Road |
| | York Road, Thirsk | Poughkeepsie |
| | North Yorkshire, YO7 3BX | NY 12601 |
| | UK | USA |

**PAYMENT** (Please tick currency you wish to use):

☐ £ (Sterling)    ☐ $ (US)    ☐ $ (CAN)    ☐ € (Euros)

Allow for shipping costs charged per order plus an amount per book as set out in the tables below:

CURRENCY/DESTINATION

|  | £(Sterling) | $(US) | $(CAN) | €(Euros) |
|---|---|---|---|---|
| **Cost per order** | | | | |
| UK | 1.50 | 2.25 | 3.50 | 2.50 |
| Europe | 3.00 | 4.50 | 6.75 | 5.00 |
| North America | 3.00 | 3.50 | 5.25 | 5.00 |
| Rest of World | 3.00 | 4.50 | 6.75 | 5.00 |
| **Additional cost per book** | | | | |
| UK | 0.50 | 0.75 | 1.15 | 0.85 |
| Europe | 1.00 | 1.50 | 2.25 | 1.70 |
| North America | 1.00 | 1.00 | 1.50 | 1.70 |
| Rest of World | 1.50 | 2.25 | 3.50 | 3.00 |

PLEASE SEND CHEQUE OR INTERNATIONAL MONEY ORDER
payable to: HOUSE OF STRATUS LTD or HOUSE OF STRATUS INC. or card payment as indicated

STERLING EXAMPLE

Cost of book(s):. . . . . . . . . . . . . . . . . . . . . Example: 3 x books at £6.99 each: £20.97

Cost of order: . . . . . . . . . . . . . . . . . . . . . Example: £1.50 (Delivery to UK address)

Additional cost per book:. . . . . . . . . . . . . Example: 3 x £0.50: £1.50

Order total including shipping:. . . . . . . . . . Example: £23.97

VISA, MASTERCARD, SWITCH, AMEX:

☐ ☐ ☐ ☐ ☐ ☐ ☐ ☐ ☐ ☐ ☐ ☐ ☐ ☐ ☐ ☐ ☐ ☐ ☐ ☐

Issue number
(Switch only):            Start Date:            Expiry Date:

☐☐☐            ☐☐/☐☐            ☐☐/☐☐

Signature:  _____

NAME:  _____

ADDRESS:  _____

COUNTRY:  _____

ZIP/POSTCODE:  _____

Please allow 28 days for delivery. Despatch normally within 48 hours.
Prices subject to change without notice.
Please tick box if you do not wish to receive any additional information. ☐

House of Stratus publishes many other titles in this genre; please check our
website (**www.houseofstratus.com**) for more details.